# ASYLUM

## By
## GINA AMOS

ISBN : 978-0-9923105-6-1

Kara Group Pty Limited
PO Box 277
Hunters Hill NSW 2110 Australia
ht@kara.com.au

TO TONI AND SEAN

Fellow writers and good friends

'The world breaks everyone, and afterward, some are strong at the broken places.'

Ernest Hemingway

# ONE

THE GROUNDS OF THE HOSPITAL for the insane were deserted. Patrick Hill pulled his yellow beanie down low over his ears and continued on his usual route, turning every now and again to see if the dog was following him. The squelching of his boots and the buzz of a lone streetlight were the only sounds. He turned his back to the wind. Winter had been reasonable up until a week ago, before the temperature dropped sharply and the rain began. For God's sake Brian, where are you? It served him right of course; he should have put the dog on the lead.

Patrick whistled once, short and sharp. The dog appeared, circled around to its left, vanished, and, seconds later, reappeared in the car park. A flash of white and then he was gone.

Patrick walked across the car park and into the courtyard beyond. On the ground lay something that looked like a bundle of old rags. The dog growled: vicious and deep. Patrick crouched down on the muddy ground and patted the dog's shoulder. 'What is it boy?' He aimed his torch to where Brian's snout was pointed.

'What's that?' He stepped back. The torch tumbled from his hands and fell to the ground. 'Sweet Jesus.'

# TWO

DETECTIVE JILL BRENNAN TOOK HER eyes off the road and glanced across at Detective Inspector Rimis. He'd been unusually quiet since they'd left the station fifteen minutes earlier. Having worked together on previous cases, the two of them were usually relaxed around each other.

'Everything all right, boss?'

Rimis leaned forward and fiddled with the heater. 'Rotten night to be out.'

Jill knew it wasn't the bad weather Nick Rimis had on his mind. He'd been grumpier than usual these past couple of days. Gossip moved quickly at the station and talk was rife with the news his ex-wife had given birth to her first child. Fiona Rimis had left the force after ten years of service. Six months later she'd left Nick Rimis after six years of marriage. She'd moved in with a younger man with a regular job, a good salary and a large house.

The tyres hissed as Jill turned the car west off Victoria Road into Darling Street. The traffic slowed. Ahead of them taillights glowed red. An accident. They didn't have time for this. She flicked the indicator, pulled out from the line of traffic and made a sharp right turn into Callan Park.

After they passed through a set of tall wrought iron gates, the car crawled along a dark, narrow ribbon of road. About three hundred metres further on, Jill slowed the car at a roundabout. An officer wearing a fluro, high-vis vest pointed a strobe to the left. When the road opened up Jill caught a glimpse of a derelict brick building, its windows boarded with thick plywood.

Rimis looked out through the windscreen. 'A lonely place.'

Jill thought the same, until she saw a burst of flashing blue and red lights ahead. She turned into the car park and pulled up next to two police vehicles. Before she turned off the ignition she glanced across at the temperature reading on the dashboard — four degrees Celsius.

Rimis unbuckled his seat belt and grabbed a pair of rubber boots from the back seat. Jill adjusted her rain jacket, pulled back on her ponytail.

'Come on, Brennan, get a move on. It's not a fashion show.' The detective inspector got out of the car, turned up his collar and started off in the direction of the police cordon tape, leaving Jill to follow.

Jill opened the car door and stepped in a puddle of mud. She swore under her breath, stared down at her shoes. Why had Rimis asked for her and not Luke Rawlings? Two more hours and her shift would have been over, another three, and she would have been at home tucked up in a warm bed. A gust of wind stung her cheeks and made her eyes water. With the wind came the smell of rain…she zipped her jacket to her chin and squelched her way after Rimis. As if on cue, a curtain of drizzle descended. She spotted Rimis standing beside a uniformed officer and a small group of onlookers huddled beneath umbrellas.

But instead of going over to him she stopped behind the ambulance. The doors were wide open and inside a paramedic strapped an oxygen mask over a man's nose and mouth. A police officer was by the old man's side, offering reassurance.

'Brennan. Over here.'

Jill turned her head and jammed her hands in her jacket pockets. She hurried over to Rimis and flashed her warrant at the uniform before signing the log. The crime-scene tape fluttered in the wind.

'That's all we need,' Rimis said, looking past Jill.

Jill turned her head to where Rimis was looking. The passenger door of a news van slid open and a woman with movie-star qualities stepped out. She was a blonde with big hair, big breasts, big mouth, dressed in a white ski jacket and a pair of black leggings tucked into knee-high leather boots. Within seconds a crew of technicians was unloading equipment.

'Come on, let's go. The last thing I feel like is talking to Katrina Andrel.'

Together they ducked beneath the crime-scene tape and marched towards the clock tower. Arc lights had been set up and the harsh white light shone in their faces.

Sydney's heavy and persistent rain during the past week had turned the grass to mud.

Jill checked her shoes. 'Should have worn boots.'

'Too late to be worrying about that now,' Rimis said. They were about to step into the improvised tent when a uniform appeared in front of them.

'Sir? Constable Jason Patullo.' The constable's nose was red from the cold; his slick, black hair plastered his forehead. 'My partner and I were the first on the scene.'

Rimis looked at him. 'I hope neither of you touched anything.'

'We were careful, sir. We only walked into the courtyard far enough to confirm it was a body and then we secured the scene.' Patullo was at least ten centimetres shorter than Rimis and built like a boxer. He couldn't have been more than twenty-five years old.

'I suppose you already know the deceased is one of us.' Patullo paused, lowered his voice. 'I found his warrant card when I went through his wallet.'

'Yeah, I know,' Rimis said.

It all made sense now. It explained why Rimis had been called out and why the television news team had been so quick to arrive. Jill looked at them both, wondered why Rimis hadn't mentioned it.

'Who found the body?' Rimis asked.

'Patrick Hill. An old guy.' Patullo blew into his cupped hands.

'What in God's name was he doing wandering around Callan Park in the middle of the night?'

'Walking his dog, sir.'

Rimis shook his head. 'If I had a dollar for every dog walker who found a dead body I wouldn't be half as worried as I am about my retirement fund,' Rimis said. 'So, what did Mr Hill have to say for himself?'

'That Brian found him.'

'Brian?'

'Yeah, his dog. Doesn't keep him on a lead; that's why he got away. Mr Hill followed him into the court-yard. The dog found the body over there by the tower.'

Rimis looked at Brennan. 'What do you think?'

'If you had a dog, would you walk him on a night like this?'

'Depends,' Rimis said.

'On what?'

'On how much I liked the dog, and how much I liked to walk at night.'

Jill half rolled her eyes and turned back to Patullo. 'Don't suppose he saw anybody hanging about?'

Patullo shook his head. 'He said all he was thinking about was finding Brian and going home to a warm bed.'

'Can't say I blame him,' Jill said.

'Brian. Bloody stupid name for a dog, don't you think?' Rimis said. 'Whatever happened to good old-fashioned names like Buddy or Rover?'

Patullo shrugged, looked down at his boots.

'What time did Mr Hill say he found the body?' Rimis asked.

'Ten-forty seven.'

Rimis raised his eyebrows. 'How can he be so sure of the time?'

'I asked him the same thing. Said he'd just checked his watch. The man's a creature of habit; he walks Brian the same time, same route, every night.' Patullo cleared his throat. 'You know the type, sir.'

'Yeah, I know the type, Constable,' Rimis said in a tired voice. Rimis dragged back the blue tarp and turned to Patullo. 'Wait here. Nobody comes in without my say so, you got that?'

'Yes, sir.'

Inside the tent, the glow of the lights and the wind flapping against the walls reminded Jill of camping holidays with her father: happy times.

Rimis rubbed his hands together, gave the police photographer a nod before he turned his attention to Doctor Ross. 'Not a good night to be out.'

'I won't argue with you there, Inspector. I can think of at least a dozen places I'd rather be.'

The camera shutter clicked in quick succession as the photographer stepped around the body. Rimis dropped to a crouch on the plastic sheeting while Jill took a step closer so she could look over Rimis's shoulder.

It was the legs that hit Jill first — bones sticking through blood-soaked jeans. Then the muddied grey-ribbed jumper. It was draped in an odd way. And the shoulders, there was something strange about them. They were narrower than they should have been. Jill ran her eyes upward to the face. She stepped back and held a closed fist to her mouth.

'Looks like he landed feet first,' Doctor Ross said in a quiet voice. 'Then rotated backwards. The tibia and fibula are fractured on both legs, the patellas would have exploded on impact.'

'What about the head wound?' Rimis asked.

'It looks like it happened during the peri-mortem period, seconds or maybe minutes before death. It takes time for blood to seep into and spread through the tissues. He could have struck his head on the side of the tower just before or after he fell.'

'Would he have been unconscious when he hit the ground?' Rimis asked.

Doctor Ross nodded. 'It's unlikely he would have suffered.'

Jill let out a soft groan and her tongue pressed itself against the roof of her mouth. Her stomach heaved. Her universe had shifted in a matter of minutes. She had to slow it down and try to make sense of what was in front of her.

Rimis looked over his shoulder. 'You alright, Brennan?'

Jill didn't know how to answer him. Her teeth clenched so hard her jaw ached. She managed a vague nod.

The photographer began to pack up his cameras and video equipment. 'I want you to take some shots of the cars parked in the surrounding streets,' Rimis said. 'Someone may have seen something.'

'What? In this weather?'

'It's only a few streets.'

The photographer slung his camera gear over his shoulder and stalked out.

Rimis turned back to Doctor Ross. 'Let's start with time of death.'

'It's not an exact science.'

'Take a guess,' Rimis said.

Doctor Ross got to her feet, snapped off her blue nitrile gloves and shoved them in a plastic bag. 'Best guess?' She stared into his eyes. 'I applied Moritz's formula and with rigor mortis unfixed, I'd say more than four but less than six hours. I'll narrow the time down once I get him on the table and examine his stomach contents.'

Rimis checked his watch.

Jill blinked. Looked at Rimis.

'You sure you're okay, Brennan?'

'I'm fine.'

'You don't look fine to me.'

How to put it? Rimis and Doctor Ross were looking at her now.

'I know him. I mean, well, knew him.' Jill held back the bitter taste in her mouth, called up an image of Robbie; saw the dimple on his cheek, his bright blue eyes, his crooked nose broken while surfing. 'It's…' she struggled with the words. 'It's Robbie Calloway. Senior Constable Robert Calloway.' And then she remembered the missed call and the voicemail message from two days ago.

When Robbie had phoned she'd been interviewing the owner of a service station after he'd reported an armed robbery attempt. She'd accidentally deleted Robbie's message but had made a mental note to call him when she got back to the station — but the call had slipped her mind.

A gust of wind shook the tarp and what had been a drizzle moments earlier, turned to a downpour.

The tent flap pushed to one side. It was Patullo. He stepped inside, shook himself and pulled back the hood of his rain jacket. 'The body snatchers are here, sir.'

They were giants of men. They stepped in and unfolded a plastic body bag. Jill put her hand to her mouth, pushed past them and ran from the tent. Rimis went to go after her, but Doctor Ross grabbed his arm and shook her head. 'Leave her.'

Doctor Ross picked up her medical bag then nodded to the two men signaling the body was ready for them.

'I don't know about you,' Rimis said to Doctor Ross, 'but I could do with some fresh air.'

Doctor Ross and Rimis joined Constable Patullo and ran towards the nearest building to take cover from the rain. The stone buildings were linked by a series of verandahs fringed by grassy courtyards. The doctor stomped her feet and dislodged clumps of mud on the flagstones. The rain poured down with renewed vigour and hammered the corrugated iron roof above them.

Rimis ran his hand through his wet hair. 'So, Doctor Ross, are we looking at suicide, here?'

'It's difficult to say. The method of death in a fall like this is hard to determine without witnesses.'

The gush of water running through the copper downpipes made conversation difficult. Rimis strained to hear her and leaned in closer. 'So you're not going to be able to tell me if he fell, jumped or if he was pushed?'

'That's exactly what I'm saying, Inspector. To prove a fall is homicidal in nature is rare.'

Rimis looked up at the tower through the rain.

Patullo interrupted his thoughts. 'Sir, I think you should know Katrina Andrel was snooping about, trying to get a story.'

Rimis narrowed his eyes. 'Hope you didn't talk to her.'

Patullo shook his head. 'No, sir.' Patullo glanced around and leaned in closer to Rimis. Patullo gave a sly smile. 'Katrina looks even better in person than she does on the telly, don't you think, sir?'

'Yes, well, Katrina Andrel can be very charming when she wants information but don't let her fool you, Constable. I wouldn't trust the woman as far as I could throw her.'

Rimis looked around for Jill. He spotted her sitting amongst the shadows at the far end of the covered walkway.

Jill got to her feet when she saw Rimis approach and straightened her back like a small child caught doing something wrong. 'Sorry, boss, I'm okay now. It was just the shock of seeing Robbie like that.'

Rimis put a hand on her shoulder. 'I'm sorry, Jill. I had no idea you knew him. Under the circumstances, anyone would have reacted the way you did.'

Jill nodded. One of the first things she'd learnt at Goulburn Police Academy was to avoid emotional involvement in a case; hard to do when the deceased was someone you knew. She thought about what Doctor Ross had said: Robbie hadn't suffered. That was something at least.

A chilly wind blew in from Iron Cove Bay, blowing thin strands of Jill's blonde hair across her face. The roof above them began to leak and heavy droplets of water slid down her back. She shivered and pulled up the collar of her jacket.

'Let's go.' Rimis motioned Jill back towards Doctor Ross and Patullo. 'Patullo, find something warm for Detective Brennan, will you? She's soaked to the bone.'

'Yes, sir.' Patullo dragged his hands out of his armpits and rushed off.

'Will you be doing the autopsy, Doctor Ross?' Rimis asked.

'It's not my decision to make. He'll be put on the routine schedule, which means you could be waiting anything up to five days for a result.' Doctor Ross wrapped her woollen scarf tighter around her neck. 'I can't wait any longer for this rain to stop. I'm going home. I've been working since four this morning.'

Rimis watched her run back to the car park; she was like a ghost moving through the dappled shadows. There was something about Greer Ross. Perhaps it was her ebony hair, or the way her hips swayed when she walked, something Rimis had noticed when he'd first met her during the Freddie Winfred case.

'Call me!' Rimis said.

She raised a hand and was gone.

Patullo returned a few minutes later with a space blanket and two umbrellas. Jill draped the blanket around her shoulders.

Rimis placed his hands on his lower back and arched slightly.'I want a word with Mr Hill.' Rimis grabbed an umbrella from Patullo and made for the ambulance with Jill and Patullo in tow.

'We're taking Mr Hill to the hospital, he's not in any state to answer questions,' the paramedic shouted to Rimis through the rain. 'He's in shock and he suffered a heart attack a few months back. We can't afford to take any chances with him.' The paramedic slammed the ambulance door shut, and with his head down he ran around to the driver's door.

'What about the dog?' Rimis asked.

'One of your officers called a local vet. The vet said he'd look after him until Mr Hill's released from hospital.' The paramedic jumped in behind the wheel and the ambulance slowly moved away.

'Let's get out of this rain,' Rimis said. They found cover under an awning of the nearest building. Rimis looked at Patullo and shook his umbrella. 'Have you got an address for the deceased?'

'Yes, sir.' Patullo stomped his feet and blew into his hands.

'Well?'

'He lives here.'

'What do you mean, he lives here?'

'I didn't mean in the grounds. He lives over in Glover Street, on the other side of the park. It's only a short walk from here.'

'Next of kin?' Rimis asked.

'He's got a sister,' Jill said.

Rimis glanced at Jill, hesitated, turned back to Patullo. 'What about a suicide note?'

'No sign of one. Forensics checked the tower. All they found was a Dolphin torch, a backpack and a navy rain jacket.'

'What was in the backpack?' Rimis asked.

'His wallet, a mobile phone, a set of keys.'

'We'll want to check out the tower and his accommodation. Now I'm wide awake, I might as well take a look at both.' Rimis turned to Brennan. 'I'll get Patullo to drive you home.'

'No, I'd rather stay.'

'You sure?' Rimis said.

Jill looked up at him and nodded. 'I'm sure.'

'What should I do now, sir?' Patullo asked.

'Best thing you can do is get that lot over there to go home.' Rimis jerked his head toward the onlookers, still braving the miserable weather.

Jill tried to put herself in Robbie's shoes, tried to picture what had happened. She imagined Robbie making his way across the car park to the tower, splashing through muddy puddles. Was he being chased? Was he pushed from the tower?

Did he fall, or did he jump? The icy wind changed direction. It looked like he'd jumped — landed feet first Doctor Ross had said. But it made no sense to her. Robbie? Top himself? No, there was no way she was buying it. Then she remembered...there was something important she had to tell Rimis.

After Patullo walked off, Jill spoke to the detective inspector in a soft voice. 'Boss, there's something you should know.'

Rimis looked to be deep in thought.

Jill took a breath and tried to block the image of Robbie's broken body.

Rimis turned to her. 'What is it?'

'Robbie was scared of heights.'

Rimis frowned. 'If he was scared of heights what the hell was doing up in the tower, then?'

'That's exactly what I was thinking.'

Rimis thumbed the switch of his Maglite and directed the torch skywards towards the tower. The beam of light caught the teeming rain in its field.

'Brennan, you've been in this job long enough to know, desperation is a powerful motivator.' Rimis paused. 'You must be…well, seeing him like that must have been…'

Jill bit her lip. The last thing she wanted was Nick Rimis's sympathy. In the Chatswood detectives' office she and Jenny Choi were the only female officers. Men dominated the ranks and that meant she had to out-perform them. Jill Brennan had paid her dues. She knew how to handle herself after years on the street up at the Cross. She could also shoot as well as the best of them, but it didn't seem to make any difference. Neither did her first-class honours degree in law or the fact she topped her graduating class at the academy or passed her detective's course with distinction.

Rimis reached into his pocket and pulled out a pack of mints. 'Want one?'

'Thanks.' Jill pushed a mint up with her thumb and popped it into her mouth.

Tell me about him,' Rimis said.

'We met at the Academy.' Jill looked him in the eye, knew he was after more, but that was all she was prepared to give him for now.

The rain abated.

'Detective Inspector? Can we get a few words from you on what happened here tonight? I understand the deceased was a police officer.'

Rimis turned around. Katrina Andrel shoved a microphone in his face. Rimis had been caught off-guard. 'Christ, Katrina. Where did you come from?'

'It will only take a minute, Nick.'

'We're very busy right now.'

'Can you at least give me a name?'

'The family hasn't been informed and you know as well as I do, we can't release a name to the public until then.'

Katrina Andrel was a piranha, a glammed-up ambitious bloodsucker. No morals, no principles, just the exclusive; end of story. Rimis knew the media had its uses, but not tonight.

Rimis gave Andrel a look that matched the weather. 'I'm sure the commissioner will hold a press conference first thing tomorrow morning. I'm afraid you'll have to wait until then.' He gave a dismissive nod, but Andrel didn't take the hint.

'What do you think about the rise in suicides in the police force and emergency services?'

She could ask all she wanted but he wasn't about to make any comment. And he knew what the stats were based on coronial cases. He knew the number of police officers, paramedics and fire fighters who took their own lives had increased over the past few years.

'No comment, Katrina.' Rimis turned his back on her. It was just like the woman to sensationalise a tragic situation. 'Come on, Brennan,' Rimis pulled up the hood of his jacket and looked back at Andrel. 'It's too cold to be standing here in the mud.'

Jill and Rimis made their way over to where the crime-scene officers were working. They were packing up, taking down the arc lights and folding up the cords. Jill recognised Senior Sergeant Hammond amongst them. He'd been a close friend of her father's and she remembered playing with his daughter when they were both children. The girl, whose name escaped her, had her father's red hair and pale complexion. Jill pulled the blanket from her shoulders and scrunched it into a tight ball.

'Hello, Jilly.' Sergeant Hammond stopped a few steps away. 'Lovely evening.' Hammond gave a hearty laugh but then leaned in, more serious. 'I heard on the grape vine you'd made detective. Mickey would have been proud of you.'

'I like to think so, Uncle Phil. But you know what Dad thought about me joining the force.'

'Yeah, I remember, but I can't say I blamed him. If my Mel had wanted to join up, I would have tried to talk her out of it.' He stared down at Jill's shoes, covered in mud. 'You should have worn your boots.'

Jill saw the look on Rimis's face and resisted the urge to give him an elbow to the ribs.

'What are your first impressions?' Rimis asked Hammond.

'Lonely spot like this?' Hammond scratched his head. 'It's got all the signs of a suicide jumper, I'm afraid.' He raised his eyebrows. 'And Callan Park of all places.'

Rimis gave a nod. 'Prints?'

'We didn't find much, not surprising with the weather the way it's been over the past week and more rain expected tomorrow. But we did find a partial footprint on the first step leading up to the tower. Looks like it matches the deceased's shoes. We'll know for sure when we get them back to the lab.'

'What about the door lock?'

'No prints there, either. But he was wearing gloves. We don't know how he got into the tower because the lock was intact. He must have had a key, unless it was already open.'

'Anything else?' Rimis asked.

'There was one thing. I found these, but I don't know what to make of them.' He held up an evidence bag.

Jill took the bag from Phil Hammond. Inside were three white feathers, but they didn't look like they were from any bird she'd ever seen. They were downy, white, looked man-made and no bigger than a fifty-cent piece.

# THREE

Rimis and Jill trekked back across the car park to the clock tower and ducked under the police tape. Jill handed the rolled up space blanket to a uniform and followed Rimis into the tower. The air was cold and dank, the smell of rats and mice fading away under years of dust. Rimis pulled the hood of his rain jacket back and raised his torch to shoulder level. They both swept their torches across the walls and up and down the narrow stairwell. Jill waited a moment for her eyes to adjust. White rivulets streaked the walls and leaf litter and dry twigs scattered the floor. The place was thick with cobwebs. Rimis pushed aside a spider's web with one hand, gripped the wrought-iron banister with the other.

'Hate spiders. What about you, Brennan?'

'I don't have a problem with them as long as I can see them. It's cockroaches I don't like. Just looking at them makes my skin crawl.'

'And here I was thinking you were fearless,' Rimis said.

Jill knew she was anything but fearless. She stopped on the stairs, grabbed the balustrade, smooth from countless hands over countless years. Her heart was racing and the walls were crowding in on her.

'Brennan where are you?' Rimis called from further up the stairs.

Jill took a deep breath, called out to him, her voice controlled. 'Coming, boss. I'll see you at the top.' She waited out the anxiety attack and minutes later the moment had passed. She continued up the stairs and at the end of the climb, she stepped into a pool of rank rainwater. Rimis was standing by the double arches, leaning out over the ledge. Jill walked up to him and stood beside him, but she couldn't look down. Instead, she looked out across the bay. She heard the boats strain against their moorings. The Parramatta River was a full, five-hundred-metre-wide streak ruffed up with waves almost a metre high. On the opposite bank, the lights of Drummoyne were barely visible through the rain. They had a closer look around, but there was nothing worth noting so they headed down.

They walked out from the tower and into the courtyard. The showery drizzle had stopped. Jill's nose had started to run and she brushed the cuff of her rain jacket under her nose. She remembered the stories she'd heard about Callan Park when she was at the Academy. With institutions like Callan Park closing, the police had become de-facto mental healthcare workers. The result? Nuffies. She had seen a lot of them up at the Cross; the land of the lost. Living on the streets, recycled over and over again through the criminal justice system with no long-term solution in sight. Jill massaged the knots in her neck and watched Rimis struggle with his torch. It kept flickering on and off. After he rapped the head of it against the palm of his hand a few times, the beam shone brighter.

Watching Rimis's torch flickering made Jill think of a B-grade horror movie. She shivered, regretted she'd been so quick to hand back the space blanket.

Jill paced around the patch of ground where Robbie's body had landed. 'What is this place, anyway?' Rimis asked. 'Jill?'

'Sorry. What did you say?'

'I asked you about this place.'

Jill looked over at him, not exactly in the mood to give a history lesson. Especially when the history was marked by questionable treatments and callous approaches to mental illness. Still, it might stop her from seeing Robbie's body... lifeless, broken. Callan Park with many of the buildings condemned for demolition was in a state of flux as local residents and Leichhardt Council fought with the state government over the property and its future usage.

Jill took a breath and pulled her coat tight around herself. 'Callan Park Lunatic Asylum was Australia's largest public works project of the nineteenth century. Sydney University leases it now from the state government.'

Rimis looked up at the tower. 'Wonder what that ball up there is.'

'There's an underground water reservoir beneath the tower. The ball rises and falls depending on the level of the water in the tanks.'

'How come you know this stuff?'

'I took a class on early Australian architecture at university. I came here sometimes to sketch the buildings.'

'You sketch? Any other hidden talents I should know about?'

She shook her head, sighed and took in the sandstone buildings. 'All these renovated buildings you see are part of the Kirkbride block. They were named after an American physician and asylum superintendent.'

'Go on,' Rimis said.

'Kirkbride came up with a design for asylums based on the principles of Florence Nightingale. Florence Nightingale thought gardens, open walkways, sunlight and fresh air were important in a patient's recovery.' Jill looked at the exterior of the buildings decorated with extravagant stone carvings. She wondered why good intentions often had the habit of turning into disappointment.

'What happened to all the patients?'

'The last of them were transferred to Concord Hospital in 2008.'

A beat of silence.

'I don't suppose they call them lunatic asylums anymore?'

It was too dark for Jill to read Rimis's expression. 'No, and they don't call them lunatics either.'

# FOUR

DAVID CHEUNG REVERSED HIS SHINY black BMW out of his driveway. He drove down the street, adjusted the rear-view mirror and glanced back at his house; three storeys of glass, marble and steel. It had taken eighteen months and three million dollars to build on the side of a sharp cliff in Northbridge, an affluent suburb on the lower north shore of Sydney, seven kilometres north of the central business district.

He came to a set of traffic lights, stopped on the amber and thought about his now-empty safety deposit box and the locked leather case beside him on the passenger seat. He was about to become two hundred thousand dollars poorer, but at least his family would be safe.

This morning he'd gone online and booked two one-way tickets to Hong Kong. The Qantas flight was leaving at 11:35 tonight and his wife had promised she and their son would be on it.

Constable Delaney looked at his watch, adjusted his Kevlar vest. 'We've got about an hour and a half until our shift ends. Wanna go down to that noodle place at the Interchange and grab something to eat?'

'Sounds good,' Constable Troy Baker said. 'But first I want to do a drive-by Douglas Avenue and see if those kids turned the music down like we asked them to. Don't want to have to deal with another complaint from the neighbours.'

Five minutes later, the highway patrol car pulled into Douglas Avenue in North Chatswood. The street was quiet. The party was over.

'Hey, look.'

'What?' Delaney wondered what Baker had seen.

'Pull over.'

'What?'

'I said pull over.'

Delaney slowed down.

'That BMW there.' Baker pointed to the car. 'There's something odd about it, look at the way it's parked.'

Delaney moaned. 'All right, but can we be quick about it? My stomach's doing backflips.' He stopped the patrol car alongside the Beemer.

They reached for their torches, got out of the car and walked up to the BMW. Delaney tried the doors first. They were unlocked. There was a briefcase and a mobile phone on the passenger seat.

'Why would anyone walk off with their phone on the seat and the car unlocked?' Baker said.

Delaney shrugged. 'Maybe the car broke down.'

'They'd ring for road-side assistance and wait in the car, wouldn't they?' Baker picked up the phone with gloved hands. 'The phone's got plenty of battery left on it.'

Delaney gave another shrug. 'Joy-riders? Kids from the party?'

'Better run a check; see if it's been reported stolen.' Baker walked around the car, inspecting it for damage. The driver's side wing was smashed and the headlamp glass was shattered. Delaney went back to the patrol car and entered the license plate number into their in-car data terminal. He waited. The car was clean. He joined Baker back at the Beemer.

'No report of it being stolen,' Delaney said. 'Now can we go and eat?' He shivered, the cold and damp biting through his clothes.

'There's something fishy about this,' Baker said. He adjusted his leather gloves and leaned into the car, pulled out the briefcase and placed it on the bonnet. After he flicked the locks, he shone his torch on loose papers, pens, and a glasses case. 'Dr David Cheung, it says here on his business card. He's an ophthalmologist, based in Victoria Avenue.'

Delaney removed a glove and placed his hand on the bonnet. 'Must have been here for a while, the motor's stone cold.'

'Did you notice it when we were here before?'

Delaney shook his head. 'No, but the street was packed with cars from the party.'

Taylor leaned into the car and grabbed the mobile phone from the passenger seat. It wasn't password protected and the last call made was to 'home.' Baker handed it to Delaney. 'See if the family knows where he is. I'll check the boot.'

Delaney walked off, made the call while his partner walked behind the car and opened the boot. He jumped back. 'Holy crap!'

Delaney ended the call and walked around to the back of the car. 'No answer on the home number.'

'Don't worry,' Baker said. 'I think I found him.'

# FIVE

JILL AND RIMIS DROVE TO the address Constable Patullo had given them for Robbie. Despite the cold, small groups of people were standing outside their homes, while others were inside making do with the view through their windows. The news van had already arrived and Katrina Andrel was interviewing the neighbours. Further down the street, the outside lights of the cottages were all on and a couple of uniforms were going from house to house.

'Shit,' Rimis said. 'How the hell did she find out Calloway's address? And she'll know his name by now after talking to that lot, if she didn't already.' Rimis released his seat belt. 'Must have been Patullo.'

'Amazing what a pair of big boobs will do,' Jill said and then climbed out of the car. She tightened her ponytail and stopped to look over to where Katrina Andrel was doing a piece to camera, standing far enough down the street to get the houses and the neighbours in the background. Jill felt decidedly short…not to mention unfeminine. Katrina Andrel appeared to be around the same age as Jill but she was taller, slimmer, had more hair and wore make-up, which was well applied.

Rimis unlatched the front gate to the rundown semi-detached cottage and walked past an overgrown front garden before taking the steps to the verandah. Jill followed. In the background Jill heard the faint rumble of traffic on Balmain Road. It was a Friday night and many people would be heading home after being out in the city.

Rimis checked if there was any sign of a break-in before he knocked on the door. Jill stood back and watched him fumble with the keys Patullo had given him. After a few attempts, he found one that fitted the lock.

Technically, this was not a crime scene, but as a precaution, they both paused to put on latex gloves. Jill kicked off her muddy shoes and slipped into a pair of paper booties. While she waited for Rimis to do the same, she realised how cold, tired and wet she felt.

Rimis fumbled for the light switch and flicked it on. The wooden floor creaked under their weight like the timbers of an old ship. They stood for a moment and took in the room. It was empty apart from a worn red lounge that looked like it had come from Vinnies. The place barely looked lived in.

'Tell me about him,' Rimis said.

'I've already told you. We met at the Academy.'

'Come on, Brennan. This is me you're talking to, remember? There's got to be more to the story than that.'

Jill sighed and unzipped her jacket. 'My first posting after I left the Academy was Darlo. A few years later, Robbie turned up there; it was a coincidence. We went out for a while but we broke up before I got my transfer to Chatswood.' Jill saw the look on Rimis's face. 'It was only a fling.'

'What else?'

'Robbie was the sort who took the job seriously, but off duty he liked to let his hair down; he was a party animal and good company until he started gambling. I'd been dating him for about four months when I first noticed a change in him. He was working too hard, doing more overtime than he needed to. One night I rang him at the station. They told me he wasn't on duty. When I asked him about it, he snapped at me, told me I had it all wrong; he wasn't working, he'd gone to the pub with his mates.'

'So his gambling was out of control?'

Jill nodded. 'It started with Keno, and then he moved onto the horses. The week before we broke up, he was on a lucky streak. He'd won over a hundred thousand dollars at Royal Randwick. A few days later, I asked him what he'd done with the money. He told me there was nothing left; he'd gambled it all away. I broke up with him that night.'

Jill wrapped her arms around herself. 'I know it sounds bad, boss, but when I saw Robbie at New Year's, he told me he had his gambling under control and I believed him. He was excited about his promotion, said he had his life together. He had plans, things to look forward to.'

'Maybe you should've gone home. You don't really need to be here, you know.'

'I know, but I'm here now so let's get this over and done with.' Jill looked across the room to a half-open door she assumed led to a bedroom. She crossed the sitting room, pushed the door open, switched the light on and walked inside. Robbie's crumpled clothing lay on the floor; a pair of faded denim jeans, a t-shirt, a pair of black-and-red-striped boxer shorts. She bent down and picked up the t-shirt from the floor, held it to her nose, took in the scent of him. She scanned the room. The queen-sized bed was unmade and there was a set of dumbbells in one corner of the room beneath the window.

On top of the chest of drawers she found a pack of unopened condoms, a betting slip for one hundred dollars on a horse called 'No Chance,' and a black comb with a few teeth missing.

'Find anything? A suicide note or a gun would help.'

'What?' Jill hadn't heard Rimis come into the room. She watched him as he got down on his hands and knees and looked under the bed.

Jill dropped the t-shirt to the floor. She wanted to tell Rimis he was wasting his time; it wasn't suicide.

'I was just on the phone to Robbie's boss, DI Perris,' Rimis said. 'Robbie's gun's missing from the station. It's not in the gun locker.'

'Well, there's nothing here.' Jill sighed. 'No note, no gun.' She walked into the second bedroom. The first thing she noticed was Robbie's laptop. When it came to computers, she knew it was best to leave it to the experts, but the Electronic Evidence Branch was notorious for its backlog. Unless it was something urgent, it always took months to get information back.

'We should get Matt to take a look at his laptop,' Jill called out to Rimis. DC Matt Chapman was the station's general dog's-body but a whiz when it came to computers. He'd been a software designer before he joined the force. Next to the laptop was a framed photo of a woman and two young children, a boy and a girl. Jill had seen the same photo at Robbie's Collaroy apartment. The woman was Robbie's grandmother. The photo had been taken in the nineties, a time when kids still played outside, built cubby houses, played Cowboys and Indians and brought home stray dogs and cats. Robbie looked to be about six or seven years old with a broad smile showing off missing front teeth. Fin, who was younger, wore a simple shift and her short hair emphasised sad, dull eyes.

Robbie and Fin had a bad start in life and Jill had often wondered how Robbie had turned out as well as he had. Children learn to survive, she thought as she reflected on her own childhood.

Jill found another photograph in the desk drawer, the edges were curled. The woman in the photograph appeared to be in her mid-to late-thirties and had a surprised expression on her face, as if the photographer had caught her unexpectedly. A strand of dark hair fell across her left cheek, her eyes were bright and excited. Jill turned it over, hoping for an inscription, but there was nothing. She looked at the photo again.

Jill knew those eyes, she'd looked into them often enough — just like Robbie's. The woman was Robbie Calloway's mother. Jill stared at the photograph for a long time and wondered if her own mother had been as happy as this woman seemed to be.

Rimis walked into the second bedroom. 'Find anything?'

'No, only some family snaps.' Jill returned the photo to the drawer and placed her hands on her hips. She looked around the room. 'Boss, there's something odd here, don't you think?'

'What do you mean?'

'Where's all Robbie's stuff? In his Collaroy apartment he had some quality furniture that belonged to his parents. I get the feeling he was just dossing down here, as if it was only a temporary arrangement.'

Rimis shrugged. 'Maybe he didn't get around to moving everything.'

Jill did a quick look around in the bathroom. It revealed nothing. The toilet seat was left up, just as you'd expect from a man living on his own. Jill walked out into the sitting room. Rimis was standing in front of the bookcase. It was filled with paperbacks and included the likes of Ian Rankin, Tess Gerritsen, PD Martin and, surprisingly, a Jamie Oliver cookbook.

Jill thought about the crime novels she'd started reading when she was a teenager and how her father had scoffed at them, told her they bore no resemblance to real-life policing.

Jill left Rimis flicking through one of Ian Rankin's books and walked into the kitchen. She opened the refrigerator and looked inside. It was home to a six-pack of beer, an out-of-date container of milk, and a few eggs. In the freezer she found frozen meat pies, an empty ice tray and a few left over slices of pizza wrapped in plastic cling wrap; pepperoni by the look of it. Inside the cupboards, white plates, white bowls, four white mugs and a half a dozen wine glasses along with a couple of battered aluminium saucepans.

Rimis came into the kitchen and opened the pantry door. 'Not much of a cook, was he?'

'He used to eat out a lot. I don't know how he managed to keep in shape with all the junk food and beer.'

A few minutes later, Jill walked out of the kitchen, across the sitting room to the window beside the front door. She pulled back the curtain; saw reflected moon-light, black sky. The news van had left and the street was now deserted. The show was over.

Across the street stood a heavy brick building with lights in some of the windows. She noticed the cars parked at odd angles in the car park and wondered where Robbie's Subaru was.

'What are you thinking?' Rimis walked up and stood beside her.

'Robbie's car. I didn't see it parked in the street. I remember when he bought it. The duco needed re-spraying and the passenger door was a different colour from the rest of the body. He spent over four thousand dollars doing it up. Robbie loved that car.

'It could be in any number of places,' Rimis said. 'In for service, someone could have borrowed it. Look, I think we've seen enough.' Rimis snapped off his gloves. 'Let's get out of here. I'll drive.'

Rimis's phone rang. It was the station. He listened, nodded and ended the call. 'Uniform's just left Fin Calloway's place. She's been told about her brother.'

Jill was silent for a moment. 'I should go and talk to her.'

'Not now, tomorrow,' Rimis said.

Jill wondered what she would say to Fin when she saw her. They didn't know anything yet. Not really.

They walked out into the street. Jill opened the passenger door, got in and turned the heater to its highest setting while Rimis plugged in his iPhone. The first track of his playlist began to play through the car's speakers. They pulled out into the street and a few minutes later the second track started.

Jill twisted in her seat and looked at Rimis. 'Are you serious, boss?'

'What?'

Jill leaned forward and wiped the fogged-up windscreen with her sleeve. 'Tony Bennett and Lady Gaga. It's a joke, right? You're trying to wind me up.'

'What's wrong with Tony Bennett and Lady Gaga?'

On the drive back to Chatswood Station, the streets were quiet. The rain and the beat of the wipers fell in time to Jill's breathing. She pressed her head back against the headrest and stared out through the windscreen.

'Any idea why he would have done it?' Rimis asked.

It? For a moment she wasn't sure what Rimis meant. Then she realised.

She looked over at him. 'No. Robbie was the most optimistic guy I've ever met.'

'When was the last time you spoke to him?'

Her breath caught.

'Jill?'

'He left a message on my phone two days ago, but I forgot to call him back.' I forgot, a pathetic excuse.

'How did he sound?' Rimis asked.

'He sounded like Robbie. Look, boss. I know what you're getting at and I know what everyone else is going to think, but I can't believe Robbie took his own life. If anything was bothering him he would have been the first person to step up and face the problem head on. Besides, he was protective of Fin. His sister was the only family he had and he wouldn't deliberately leave her on her own.'

When Rimis drove into the station car park twenty minutes later, he pulled up next to Jill's car. He looked at Jill, then her car. 'I should drive you home.'

'No need, I'm fine.'

'You should have someone with you. I can make you something to eat. I'm good at toasted cheese sandwiches. I'm also a good listener if you want.'

Jill smiled. 'I appreciate your concern, Nick, I really do, but I'll be okay. I just want to have a hot bath and go to bed.' Jill got out of the car. She fumbled with her keys, knowing Rimis was watching her. When she got her car door opened she turned and waved to him. He hesitated for a moment before he drove off.

Jill didn't know how she'd managed to drive home or how she'd climbed the stairs to her second-floor apartment. Even though she was exhausted she did her routine check of the locks before she ran a bath. After a hot soak in the tub she changed into a fleecy tracksuit and collapsed onto the bed. She stared up at the ceiling. It would be daylight soon and even though she had an early start, she couldn't sleep. She picked up her mobile phone from the bedside table and tapped on the image gallery. She flicked through her photos until she found one of Robbie. He had his arm around her at Avalon beach, a few weeks before they'd broken up. She kept struggling to find a way to make it not true. How could Robbie be dead? She dropped the phone and rolled over onto her side. She punched her pillow. It wasn't long before the tears started to flow.

# SIX

THE DREAM HAD YANKED FIN Calloway out of sleep. She rolled out of bed. The first thing she noticed was the gash on her leg. It was swollen and sore. Strange. She hadn't felt the pain until now. On her way to the bathroom she tripped on a pile of wet clothing, noticed the muddy footprints on the carpet. She had no memory of when or how she'd got home last night. This was happening to her a lot lately, gaps in her life she couldn't explain.

In the bathroom she clung to the sink with one hand, leant over and spat the bile from her mouth, splashed cold water on her face. She should shower, but she needed coffee first. She looked in the mirror, studied her face. Who are you Fin Calloway? She knew it wasn't the weight she'd put on or even her face that was puffy from crying; there was something terribly wrong with her.

When had it started? And why? The heavy drinking, the blackouts, the depression. She'd been an embarrassment to Robbie. That was why he'd never introduced her to any of his friends. She'd only met one of Robbie's friends in the past year or so — a woman called Jill Brennan. And that was only because Fin had turned up unannounced at Robbie's apartment and Jill had been there.

Fin stumbled into the kitchen and looked out the window at the quiet street outside her apartment. Sydney was waking up to another wet and gloomy day.

When she grabbed a pack of cigarettes from the kitchen counter she noticed, not for the first time, the health warning and photo of a cancerous lung on the pack. Instead of lighting up, she switched the kettle on, picked up a mug from the sink and waited for the water to boil. She closed her eyes. The darkness spread. She tried to piece together what she could remember of the dream... she'd been trying to get away from someone, or something.

# SEVEN

CHATSWOOD DETECTIVE'S OFFICE WAS IN full swing. The wheels didn't stop turning because one of their own had committed suicide. From his west-facing office on the third floor, Nick Rimis had a view onto Archer Street. He got up from his desk and walked over to the window. The street was crammed with peak-hour traffic.

Rimis hadn't slept much last night and already his face was showing the signs of a new beard. On his desk the *Sydney Morning Herald* lay open at page five. He'd just finished reading Katrina Andrel's article on Calloway's suicide. Thank God they'd managed to get a hold of his sister. What a shock it would be to find out about a loved one's death in the paper. He walked back to his desk and looked at the article again.

The death of Senior Constable Robert Calloway at Callan Park last night is not being treated as suspicious, according to police sources. The New South Wales Health Minister, Suzette Schofield, described Constable Calloway's death as a tragedy. 'In light of the increase in suicides in the emergency services, we'll be increasing funding for mental health,' she said. 'We are committed to helping those people who serve this state.'

In response to the minister's comments New South Wales Police Commissioner, Trevor Whyte, told the *Herald* the New South Wales Police Force was deeply saddened by the loss of one of its own. He encouraged his officers to seek counselling if they were personally affected by the tragedy. A representative from the 'Friends of Callan Park', Rozelle resident Mrs Dorothy Bates, urged the state government to approve the community Master Plan and return Callan Park in part, to a mental institution. Constable Calloway is survived by his sister, Fin Calloway, but she was not available for comment.

Rimis was tempted to throw the paper in the rubbish bin but instead he flipped to the back pages and found the cryptic crosswords. A distraction when he was stressed. He drummed his pen on the desk and spent a few moments thinking about a clue.

'Am I interrupting anything?'

Rimis knew the voice. DCI Scott Carver. Rimis closed the newspaper and folded in two. He pushed his chair back from his desk and got to his feet. 'No, not at all, come in. I was just reading the article in this morning's paper about Constable Calloway. Have you read it?'

'Yeah, I've read it. I knew Robbie. I haven't seen him in about three or four years. Even though he was in uniform he was the sort of guy you could talk to. Jokes, gossip and the occasional beer down at the pub.' Carver shook his head. 'I find the idea of suicide hard to believe. Robbie never struck me as the type to succumb to depression.'

'Strange you should say that. You're the second person to voice that concern.' Rimis pointed to one of the visitor chairs. 'Have a seat.'

'Who was the first?' Carver asked as he pulled at the creases of his trousers and sat down.

'Detective Brennan.'

'Jill? I wouldn't mind hearing her thoughts,' Carver said. 'Is she in?'

'I'll check.' Rimis picked up his phone and dialled her extension.


A few minutes later, Jill knocked on Rimis's open door and saw Scott Carver sitting across from Rimis.

'Come in, Brennan.' Rimis stretched back in his chair. 'DCI Carver would like to talk to you about Robbie Calloway. He wants to hear first-hand your impressions from last night.'

Carver stood up and took Jill's hand. His grip was firm, strong and warm. Their gazes held and an intense feeling flared up inside her. She tugged her hand back but he tightened his grip for a moment before he released her.

Scott Carver was slimmer than she remembered. With broad shoulders, a strong jaw and those eyes of his; eyes that made you want to look away in case he worked out what you were thinking. And she'd forgotten how tall he was. At around one hundred and ninety centimetres, his height put her at a distinct disadvantage. Scott Carver's career, like hers, had been fast-tracked. Area Commander Carver was headed for the top job one day and looking at him now she understood why; he had a strong and powerful presence.

'Detective Brennan.' He smiled as if they were sharing an inside joke. Jill felt small and compact next to him and was embarrassed by the warmth she felt in her cheeks.

'Have a seat, Brennan.' Rimis looked at her, then looked at Scott Carver. 'Am I missing something here?'

'We have mutual friends,' was all Jill said. If it hadn't been for the Taggart case she'd been working on when she first met Scott Carver at a birthday party for Bea's son, she would have given into Bea's nagging and gone out with him.

Jill sat down. She wasn't sure why she'd been called to Rimis's office. If it was about what happened last night at Callan Park, surely Rimis could have told Scott Carver the details.

'I hear you don't think Robbie Calloway's death was suicide? Why?'

Jill looked at Rimis, then back to Carver. She adjusted her ponytail. 'I've known Robbie Calloway for many years. We were at the Academy together and in all that time I never knew him to be depressed about anything. He was always upbeat and confident. I'm sure he would have told me if there was anything bothering him.'

'Have you read the newspaper this morning?' Carver asked.

'Not yet, but I caught the segment on Robbie on *The Morning Show* before I came into work.'

'I heard you'd been in a personal relationship with him. It must have been a terrible shock for you,' Carver said.

'Yes it was.' Seems news, or more like gossip, travelled fast. And now it was Scott Carver, of all people, talking about her relationship with Robbie. She was silent, staring at the cup of coffee on Rimis's desk and wishing she could get her own caffeine fix...or maybe something stronger.

Carver shifted in his chair. 'I know it's been less than twenty-four hours, but are you following any leads to suggest his death was anything other than suicide?'

Jill was relieved to focus on the case.

Rimis said, 'I think —'

Jill cut him off. 'There's a CCTV camera in the western car park not far from where Robbie's body was found. It could be useful in telling us what happened last night. I've been onto the security company this morning and they told me the camera was only installed a few days ago after some of the university staff had their cars vandalised. I'm going to see them later this morning and take a look at the tapes.'

Carver leaned back in his chair. 'Good idea, the tapes might shed some light on Calloway's movements and death.'

'What about the door knocks?' Carver asked Rimis.

Rimis shook his head. 'They weren't much help. Everyone was either out or at home watching the footy.'

'I called all the local real estate agents in the area,' Jill said. 'And when I finally got onto the managing agent for the property in Glover Street, they told me Robbie only moved in a couple of weeks ago. But here's the interesting thing,' Jill shifted to the edge of her chair, 'he only wanted to sign a lease for three months. Apparently he was pretty pissed off when the agent insisted on a six-month lease.'

'What can you tell me about the sister?' Carver asked.

'I'm going to see her this morning after I've finished at the security company.'

'You're wasting your time on this, Brennan. There's no doubt in my mind it was suicide,' Rimis said.

'Maybe Detective Brennan should follow her instincts on this one, Nick. After all, she did know him better than any of us.'

For a few moments nobody spoke. It was Carver who broke the silence. He looked at his watch. 'I've got a meeting in North Sydney in half an hour, I should be going.' He got to his feet and looked at Jill. 'Let me know what you find on the CCTV. With no witnesses, it might hold the key to what happened last night.'

'Yes, sir.' Jill stood up.

Scott paused, looked at Jill. 'Robbie was a bloody good cop. He'll be missed.'

Rimis got to his feet to see Scott Carver out and Jill went back to her desk.


Five minutes later Rimis stormed down the corridor towards the detectives' room. 'Brennan!' Rimis roared her name so loud, the whole station shook. 'In my office, now!'

Jill hurried down the corridor, barely managing to keep it together. What was wrong with the man?

'Come in and close the door.' Rimis slumped down in his chair. 'For Christ's sake, Detective, what did you think you were playing at?'

The use of the word detective had the same effect on her as when she called Rimis, sir. Nick Rimis was seriously pissed off with her for some reason.

'Sit down!'

Jill adjusted herself in the chair, straightening up for whatever was coming.

'I'm only going to have this discussion with you once,' he began. 'You're part of a team. You're an intelligent woman and I know I don't have to give you the definition of team. You just can't go off half-cocked every time you come up with an idea based on some crazy hunch you might have.' Rimis was pacing a short track on the carpet behind his chair.

Jill had only seen Rimis like this once before, when Rawlings had stood in a pool of blood at a crime scene. She knew it was best not to say anything and to wait for him to calm down.

Rimis walked over to the window. He had his hands clasped behind his back and she could hear him swearing under his breath. A few moments later, he turned around. His face had almost returned to its normal colour.

'The Commissioner is on the warpath. The media is hounding me.' Rimis ran his fingers through his hair. His voice dropped. 'For Christ's sake, Brennan why do you always want to make every case your personal crusade? I know you're upset over Calloway's death but you should have run it past me before you started your own investigation instead of springing it on me in front of Carver.'

'Sorry, boss. I was out of line.' So that's what this was about — she made him look bad in front of Scott.

After a few beats of silence Rimis said, 'Are you sure you don't want a couple of days off?'

'I'm fine.' She looked down at her hands in her lap. She thought Nick Rimis could do with a few days of leave himself.

Rimis frowned. 'Listen —'

Jill looked up. 'What do you want me to do? Take a day or two off, file my nails, get my hair done?'

Rimis rolled his eyes. 'Come on, Brennan, don't be a pain in the arse.'

'I can't just sit around and do nothing. If I take time off and allow myself to grieve for Robbie, I'll lose my edge. The adrenaline is the only thing that's keeping me going.' Jill rubbed her eyes. 'Robbie's dead and I know I can't do anything about that, but I need to know why he died. I owe it to him and I owe it to Fin.' Jill was about to say she owed it to herself but stopped short. She was wasting her breath. Everyone was convinced it was suicide.

Rimis walked back to his desk and sat down. 'I would never have taken you with me to Callan Park last night if I'd known the deceased was someone you knew. I thought I was doing you a favour getting you away from your desk.' Rimis lifted his coffee mug, swirled it around and examined it. 'I'll be watching you, you know.' He looked up at her. 'If I think for one second this case affects the way you perform your duties, I'll —'

'Understood, sir.' Jill got to her feet to leave.

'No need to call me, sir.' Rimis's forehead creased into a frown.

Jill tucked a strand of hair that had fallen loose from her ponytail behind her ear and headed towards the door.

'Jill?'

She stopped, turned around.

'Forget Robbie for now. I want you to go to North Shore Hospital and check on the boy who was attacked at the Train and Bus Interchange a couple of nights ago.'

'Adam Lee?' Jill had heard his name in yesterday morning's meeting. He'd been stabbed.

'Carver thinks his attack and Cheung's murder last night have something to do with these Asian gangs operating across Sydney. See if you can get the boy to give us a name or description of his attacker. And take Choi with you. Lee will be scared, but I want you to remind him what he's up against if he doesn't talk to us.' Rimis picked up a file and shook his head. 'What was it about last night? Did I miss something? Was it a full moon?' He flicked through the file on David Cheung. 'I'll have a word with Rawlings about the Cheung murder, I know it's his case but I want you two to work together on it.'

Jill nodded even though she wanted to focus on Robbie.

'Listen Jill, if you change your mind about taking leave you can —'

'Don't worry, boss. You'll be the first to know.'

'Jill we've been friends…that is, colleagues for some time now. Why don't you go away somewhere; get your head in order. Come back when you're ready. We can always arrange extra leave if you need it.'

'Is that an order?'

'No,' Rimis said, 'it's a lifeline.'

# EIGHT

RIMIS SAT BACK IN HIS chair and ran his hands down his face. Maybe he'd been too hard on Brennan. He knew first hand what it was like to go against popular opinion. In the Winfred case wasn't he the only one who'd believed Kevin Taggart was a serial killer? Everyone else had thought he was a gifted artist, including Brennan.

Brennan had been chosen for an undercover assignment into an art fraud racket in Eastern Sydney. But what had started off as a straightforward case quickly turned into a major murder and drug investigation. Rimis knew if it hadn't been for his doggedness, Jill would have been Kevin Taggart's next victim.

He could at least give Calloway's death a day or two of his team's time, for Brennan's sake. They could look into it in conjunction with their other cases. Rimis stood up from behind his desk and walked down the corridor to the detectives' room. He headed straight for Matt Chapman's workstation.

'Find anything on Calloway's laptop, Matt?'

Detective Matt Chapman sat upright removed his dark-framed glasses and put down what remained of his sandwich. He'd been looking at the laptop before Rimis had interrupted him. 'There's nothing special about it, boss. You could buy one of these at any electrical store for a good price, especially if they were on sale. Still using Windows XP, a bit slow and out-dated, but does the job well enough.' He wiped his mouth with a white napkin. 'I found a range of browsing sites, a bit of soft porn amongst it all, nothing too erotic though, no anal sex, gang bangs or threesomes. His taste was for blondes with big tits, Caucasians mainly.'

Rimis cleared his throat and shifted his feet. 'Get on with it Chapman.'

'Sorry, boss.' Matt Chapman's face reddened. He replaced his glasses and sat forward in his chair. 'If you ask me, Calloway had nothing to hide.' He tilted the computer screen back so Rimis could see it better.

'What about Facebook?' Rimis leaned towards the computer screen.

'Just the usual snaps of pretty girls, him at the beach with his surfboard,

drinking with mates, that sort of thing. A few photos of him at a racecourse, looked like Royal Randwick to me. He definitely liked to party. But there's one name that keeps popping up. Fin, no last name, no photo tag. Don't know whether they're male or female. Could be a nickname.'

Rimis crossed his arms. 'Fin's his sister.'

Chapman nodded. 'Thought you'd want to know, there are a few photos of Jill amongst them.'

Rimis raised his eyebrows. 'Nothing compromising?'

'No. All pretty innocent.'

'Anything else?'

'He visited a few chat rooms, message boards, tweeted.'

'Were there any visits to suicide sites, mental health helplines, gambling sites, that sort of thing?'

'He logged onto Beyond Blue and the Black Dog Institute forums a couple of times, but he didn't interact. He also logged on to a site called The Friends of Callan Park, and an online gambling site. As far as I could see, he didn't place any bets.'

'When did he last use his laptop?'

Chapman passed him a print of the screen capture. 'This was what he was looking at before he logged off at 7.36 pm the night he died.'

Rimis took the sheet of paper, looked at it for a moment. 'Know what it is?'

'A continental goods warehouse in Chatswood. I had a quick look at the building's paperwork but it all looks legit.'

Rimis folded the sheet in two and put it in his pocket. 'Have you had a chance to check his mobile phone and emails?'

'We've made a list of recent calls he made and received. Rawlings is going through them now, matching names and addresses. He's also checking the photos taken by the police photographer of the cars parked in Glover Street last night.' Chapman rolled his shoulders back. 'I've gone through most of his emails but there was nothing worth noting. I found some other photos, sandstone and derelict buildings, long verandahs, and grassy parklands. Also there are some photos of houses. They look like workman's cottages to me, could be in Rozelle or Balmain. I'll email copies to you, if you want.'

'Good work, Matt.'

On his way back to his office, Rimis tugged at his tie and made a mental note to clear the web browsing history from his computer.

# NINE

JILL HEADED STRAIGHT FOR THE bathroom after she left Rimis's office. She checked that none of the cubicles were occupied before she chose one at the end of the row. She sat down on the closed lid and wiped her nose with a sheet of toilet paper. She had to pull herself together. She couldn't afford to fall apart the way she had during the Kevin Taggart case, if she did, she knew questions would be asked about her ability to do her job. The job. It meant everything to her. She flushed the toilet. At the washbasin she splashed her face with cold water and looked at herself in the mirror. If only she'd returned Robbie's phone call. She couldn't stop herself from thinking that if she had, he might still be alive.

Two loud pings in succession signalled two new messages. Jill took her phone out of her pocket and read the first message. It was the security company confirming her appointment; the second was from Bea Travers. 'Heard about Robbie. R u ok?'

A few minutes later, Jill walked out of the bathroom and headed back to her desk. She logged on to her computer, checked her emails then sat back in her chair and stared at the computer screen.

Her father had once explained to her that there were two types of police officers — the ones who could go home after every shift and switch off, and the ones who could never let go. She was the latter.

She took a sip of tea. It was stone cold, but she finished it anyway. Jill clicked on Robbie's file. Questions needed answers. Sure, she was supposed to be heading to the hospital to speak to Adam Lee but a few minutes for Robbie wouldn't make any difference to anyone. She stood and glanced around the cubicles...Rawlings was at his desk next to hers but he was busy working on a report and he had his earphones in. What Rimis didn't know... She searched for the phone number for Manly Police Station, sat down at her desk, dialled and gave her name. Moments later she heard a gravelly voice on the end of the line. 'DI Perris.'

'DI Perris, this is Detective Jill Brennan from Chatswood Detectives,' Jill said in a quiet voice.

'What can I do for you, Detective?'

'I wanted to speak to you about Senior Constable Calloway; he was a very close friend.'

There was an unexpected silence down the phone.

Jill cleared her throat. 'I know this is an unusual request, sir, but I was wondering if there was anything you could tell me about the last few weeks of his working life. Was he behaving in a way that —'

'Look, I'm sorry Detective but there's nothing to tell. Senior Constable Calloway was working on a number of cases prior to his death, but nothing that would make him want to...to take his own life.'

She took a breath, but he cut her off again.

'It's obviously hard for you to accept his death, and the way it happened. I suggest you seek counselling...that's what it's there for. Now if you don't mind, I'm about to go into a meeting.'

'Oh...um, okay. Thanks for your time.' She kept the sarcastic tone out of her voice.

'You're welcome. Goodbye.' The line went dead.

Jill put down the phone. If Perris knew anything he wasn't about to share it with her. If Rimis ever found out she'd spoken to Perris, he'd read her the riot act, again. And in the end the phone call had been a complete waste of time. Jill checked the time on her phone. Adam Lee would have to wait until this afternoon.

Jill left Chatswood Station and thirty minutes later she walked through the automatic glass doors to the offices of Access Security. The receptionist asked her to take a seat. Five minutes later she was led down a corridor and into the manager's office. After the introductions, the manager handed Jill a series of photos. She laid them out in front of her on his desk and studied them. 'What? This is all you've got?'

'I'm afraid so,' he said.

'I don't mean to tell you how to do your job, but it's obvious from the quality and number of photos, the CCTV coverage on the site is grossly inadequate. I know you've got foot patrols at regular intervals, but what happened last night may have been avoided if…'

The manager raised both hands. 'I agree with you one hundred percent, Detective. I can't tell you how many discussions and meetings I've had with the university about increasing the security at Callan Park, but it's all about budgets and cost-cutting these days. There's talk the Federal Government plans to axe $2.5 billion dollars from funding to universities and student support programmes in the next budget. The reason the CCTV is there at all is because a few of the students and lecturers had their cars vandalised a few weeks ago.'

What else was there to say?

On the way back to the car park, Jill stopped and looked at the grainy photos again. They'd been printed on heavy gloss paper and showed a lone figure in a hooded tracksuit. The face was obscured and it was hard to tell if it was a man or a woman. It could be Robbie, but Jill knew there was little, if any chance of a formal identification based on these photographs.

Once she was behind the wheel, Jill threw the envelope on the passenger seat and punched Fin Calloway's address, which she'd committed to memory, into her GPS. She looked at the display. She was nine kilometres from Fin's apartment. The GPS told her she'd be there in eleven minutes.

# TEN

FIN CALLOWAY LIVED ON THE third floor of a six-storey apartment block. The lifts were out of service so Jill took the stairs to Fin's apartment. She knocked on the door, waited a full minute before she knocked again. A bolt clunked, a chain rattled and the door inched open.

'Fin? It's Jill Brennan, I was a friend of Robbie's. Can I come in?'

'What do you want?'

Jill could see Fin through the gap, silhouetted against subdued lighting. A tall figure. 'I wanted to talk to you, see how you are.' The chain was still on the door.

Fin unlinked the chain and opened the door. She stepped back. She was tall like Robbie, six feet, one hundred and eighty centimetres. Jill remembered Robbie telling her he hated it when Fin wore heels because she towered over him.

Jill immediately caught a whiff of Fin's boozy breath and sour body odour.

'Come through, I was having a drink.'

Jill trailed behind Fin down the narrow hallway past a navy rain jacket and an assortment of hats on brass coat hooks fixed to the wall. Jill noticed the clothes Fin was wearing: a long skirt and a jumper two sizes too large for her. Her feet were bare and even in bare feet, Jill felt like a midget next to her.

Fin turned the television off and poured herself a whiskey from an almost empty bottle. 'Did you see *The Morning Show*?'

'Yes,' Jill said.

'Reporters keep ringing me. I told them all to fuck off.' Fin aimed the glass in Jill's direction and sat down on a stool at the kitchen counter. 'You want one? I know you're not s'posed to drink when you're on duty. You are on duty, aren't you? That's why you're here, right?'

'I am, but even if I wasn't, I would have come. Robbie would have wanted me to be with you.'

Fin threw back the contents of the glass tumbler. Silence.

'Look, Fin, I know we've only met once, but I just wanted to say how sorry I am and if there's anything I can —'

'Yeah, yeah. I know.' Fin's face tightened. 'I've heard it all before. You think this is the first time I've lost family?' Fin made a loud sniffing sound, wiped stray tears away with her thumb.

Jill gave her a few moments. She wanted to cry with her, but held back, knowing it wouldn't do either of them any good if she broke down now. Jill rummaged around in her bag for her notebook, realised it wasn't there. It must have fallen out in the car. She sat down next to Fin and realised she hadn't even thought about the questions she was going to ask. She looked at Fin's face; it was expressionless. She tried to think of something to say, something to console her. But there was nothing.

'Grab yourself a glass.' Fin nodded towards the sink. 'Robbie always said it was never a good idea to drink alone.'

Jill was grateful for the distraction and rinsed a glass before she filled it with tap water.

Fin poured herself another shot of whiskey while Jill looked around the apartment, taking in the clothes strewn across the floor, the stains on the carpet, and a vase filled with dead tulips on the timber sideboard.

Jill took a sip of water. 'I need to ask you a few questions, Fin. I'm sorry, I really am. I wish they could wait.'

Fin massaged her temples with her knuckles.

'You don't look well,' Jill said.

'Got a headache, won't go away.'

'Can I get you something?'

'Already had half a dozen paracetamol.'

'What about a cup of tea?' Jill looked at the almost empty bottle of whiskey. No wonder Fin had a headache.

'No, I'll stick to this.' Fin raised her glass.

Jill paused, then said, 'There'll have to be an autopsy and a coroner's report.'

Fin examined her hands, searched the lines of her palms and dug her fingernails into them.

Jill persevered. 'Do you have any idea what Robbie was doing at Callan Park last night? And in the tower of all places. We both know he was scared of heights.'

'No idea. If I'd known he was going there, I would have stopped him and...' Fin banged her head on the kitchen counter.

'Sorry, Fin, I...'

Fin looked up, her forehead already red and swollen, a bruise in the making. 'Just ask yer questions, then you can piss off and leave me alone.'

Jill wondered how many whiskeys Fin had knocked back today. 'When did you last see, Robbie?'

Silence.

'A week ago.'

'Did he seem depressed or act in any way that made you think something was troubling him?'

Fin drained the whiskey in one neat gulp, slammed the glass down. It almost missed the counter. 'Could have been. He was fidgety, came for dinner, didn't eat. Knew there was something. Wouldn't tell me, would he? Thought it was because of Gracie. She died a few months back. They were close. He was missing her.'

'Your grandmother?'

Fin nodded. 'She brought us up after our parents died, we called her Gracie, better for us, she said, you know, around our friends and that. She died; she was old and sick. Sick of living more like it. Robbie said it was her time.' Fin pulled a cigarette from a crumpled pack, looked at it between her fingers. 'Gotta give these things up, as well as the drink.' Fin's hand trembled as she lit the cigarette. She held her breath for a moment before she blew the smoke out through her nose. 'Can't stop thinking about him, though, lying there in the mud. Wonder if he felt anything? Your lot told me he'd have been unconscious when he hit the ground, but they wouldn't know for sure, would they?' Fin wrapped a lock of hair around her finger. 'If I hadn't known him so well, s'pose I wouldn't have noticed the change in him. He was good at covering things up.'

'What sort of change?' Jill met Fin's eyes and could see the pain and anger there. Her world had just been torn apart and Jill knew how that felt — and understood why she wanted to drink herself into oblivion.

Fin ignored her, took a drag on her cigarette instead. Her face crumpled. 'Should have made him tell me what was going on, could have talked it through.' She threw her head back and blew smoke into the air.

'Look, Fin, I know this is difficult for you, but it would really help if we knew what Robbie was doing at Callan Park last night and why he'd moved from Collaroy.'

'Robbie? He moved? I thought he was still living in Collaroy.' Now the tears were flowing. 'What business is it of yours, anyway? It was suicide, wasn't it?'

Jill said nothing. She knew Robbie's death had all the hallmarks of suicide but she still couldn't come to grips with the idea of it.

Fin shook her head and wiped her eyes with the palms of her hands. 'It's a family matter, but then you wouldn't know about family, would you? Robbie told me you didn't have one.'

Jill shut her eyes, opened them, and picked up the glass of water, thought about adding whiskey to it. She ploughed on. 'Do you know if Robbie was gambling again?'

Fin had stopped crying. 'I wouldn't know even if he was.' Fin drew on her cigarette, tossed her head back.

Jill moved onto her next question. 'Ever heard of an organisation called The Friends of Callan Park?'

'Nope.' Fin flicked ash at a saucer then poured two fingers of whiskey into Jill's glass. She grabbed her own glass, stood up and walked over to a set of windows. The wild wind outside thrashed through the tree branches. Sheets of rain slammed into the windows.

'Quite a day out there,' Jill said as she watched Fin. She'd be on her own now, the last of her family gone. Jill knew what that felt like.

When Robbie introduced them, Jill thought Fin was cold, unfriendly, but looking at her now, she felt sorry for her.

'The last time I saw Robbie he'd just been promoted,' Jill said.

'Robbie was in a good place then.' Fin spun around, half smiled. 'He was the happiest I'd seen him since the two of you split up.' She sighed. 'But around the time Gracie died, something happened between us, don't know what it was, but he stopped calling me. No texts or emails either. I had a go at him about it, but he wouldn't tell me anything. Last week was the first time I'd seen him since Gracie's funeral.' She took another drag on her cigarette. 'Maybe there was a woman in his life, but I don't know for sure.'

'Did he mention anyone? A name you hadn't heard before?' Jill got up from the kitchen counter and crossed over to Fin. 'Try to remember Fin, it's important.'

'He might have.' She ran her hand through her greasy hair. 'Been having trouble remembering things lately.' She stared at Jill. 'You're a detective now, aren't you?'

Jill nodded.

'Robbie always said you'd go far. Said it was always the job before anything else with you.'

Jill wasn't sure what to make of that. Was it supposed to be a compliment or a criticism? She changed the topic. 'We haven't been able to find Robbie's gun. It should be locked up at the station, but it's missing. He didn't say anything to you about bringing his gun home, did he?'

'Like I said, I've only spoken to him once since Gracie's funeral. Anyway, Robbie didn't talk to me about his work. He knew it upset me.' Fin gulped down another mouthful of whiskey.

Fin looked past Jill. She seemed to be in a world of her own.

'We used to drive past the asylum when we were kids. You could see the clock tower for miles. It was on a ridge. Gracie talked about Annie Calloway, great, great something or other… she was one of the lunatics. She hanged herself from that tower. She worked in the laundry, made a rope out of bed sheets.' The ash on her cigarette was getting longer, threatening to spill onto the floor but Fin didn't seem to notice. 'Robbie and I used to nag Gracie to take us inside to see it up close, but she said the place was full of crazy people and we weren't allowed.'

Fin glanced at her cigarette and stubbed it out before continuing. 'Robbie and I played these silly games, made up stories. He called me Mad Annie and promised to take care of me, no matter what.' Fin's eyes glazed over. 'Kid's stuff. It was all just kid's stuff.' Fin returned to the counter for another cigarette and lit it.

After a couple of drags, she looked Jill up and down. 'I don't understand what you're doing here, anyway. Robbie killed himself, end of story. Shit happens.'

Jill hesitated. 'I thought you might like to see Robbie.' She lowered her voice. 'It will help you deal with your grief, accept his death. I could take you.'

At least he'd be cleaned up at the morgue, Jill thought. And Fin would just see his face. Then she'd realise he was really gone.

'Okay.' Fin's eyes brimmed with tears.

'I'll pick you up tomorrow morning. Around nine?' Fin nodded.

Jill took a breath. 'But maybe you should go easy on the whiskey?' Fin gave a non-committal nod.

'I've got one more question before I go.'

'What?'

'Where were you last night?'

Fin crinkled her brow, scrunched her face slightly. 'Here, of course.'

'Alone?'

'Yeah.' She stared into her whiskey. 'I'm always alone.'

Jill gave little nods, then said: 'I'll let myself out.' She drifted towards the front door, and then turned back. 'Fin?'

'I thought you were leaving.' Fin looked up, wiped a tear away.

Jill had been about to float a different theory…ask Fin if she thought Robbie was mixed up in something serious enough to get him killed. But the look on Fin's face stopped her.

'Take care of yourself,' Jill said instead.

She needed more facts before she pulled the grieving sister down that rabbit hole.

# ELEVEN

FIN'S MOBILE PHONE BUZZED AND made her jump. She opened her eyes, rolled off the sofa and fell onto the floor. She tried to stand. Felt sick. Far too much whiskey. Where was her phone? It had been sitting on the coffee table the last time she'd seen it. There. She reached for it; surprised the battery wasn't dead because she couldn't remember the last time she charged it. This isn't going to be good, she thought. Probably Jill Brennan checking up on her or that reporter woman again, the one who claimed she knew Robbie. She was after a human-interest story, a close-up account of a grieving sister who'd lost her copper brother to suicide. She looked at the screen. It was Adam. She hesitated then answered it.

'Fin? Fin, it's me.' His voice was panicky. 'Are you okay? I just saw Robbie on the news. Man, why'd he go and do a thing like that?'

Fin couldn't speak. Her heart thumped. The only thing she could think of was Robbie lying in the mud.

'Fin? Are you there? I know you must be freaking out. Why don't you come and see me. I could do with some visitors. I've got all these tubes in my chest. They make me look like some sort of freakin alien. They're supposed to suck the blood and air from my chest to get my lungs working again.'

Fin closed her eyes. 'Fin? You there?'

'I'm here.'

'So, you wanna come and see me?'

Fin swallowed. 'No, can't face anyone now.' She pressed the end button through a drunken fog and slumped back on the sofa.

# TWELVE

JILL TOSSED A COPY OF the forty-page report on the Red Cave Gang to one side of her desk and leaned back in her chair. Instead of concentrating on the report she'd been going over the conversation she'd had with Fin. She kept thinking about Robbie and Fin's distant relative who'd hanged herself from the tower. An eerie coincidence…what else could it be?

After she drained her fourth cup of green tea for the day she leaned back in her chair and looked at her in-tray. There was a backlog of requests from the DPP for further statements to review, call-back messages, and witness subpoenas on a cleaning business fraud case she'd been working on for the past three months.

She decided to tackle the call-back messages first, picked up the pile, but then put them aside. Thoughts of Robbie, again. Even though they were still waiting for the autopsy, Robbie Calloway was now a suicide statistic as far as Rimis was concerned.

She'd gone over and over all the things that didn't add up. Like why Robbie had moved from Collaroy on the Northern Beaches to Rozelle, to a dump. And why, within only two weeks of his moving, he'd jumped to his death from the clock tower in the grounds of Callan Park? And why would he have even gone up there when he hated heights? It didn't make sense. And there was his gun. What had happened to it?

Jill pushed back her chair and went in search of Jenny Choi. When she walked out into the corridor Jill almost collided with her. She had a bundle of files in her arms and Jill offered to help her carry them back to her desk.

Choi dumped the files on her desk. Today, Jenny Choi was wearing a denim jacket over a striped pink and white jumper, a short black skirt, black tights and red boots with heels that boosted her height so she could look most of the other detectives in the eye. Jill imagined she got away with wearing outrageous clothing because she had an almost movie-star status among the Chinese community, especially with the druggies down at the Train and Bus Interchange.

'I need to talk to you about Adam Lee,' Jill said. 'The boss wants us to go to the hospital and see if we can get a name or at least a description of his attacker from him.'

'Crap, I was planning to go through these files this afternoon.'

'Rimis said it was a priority,' Jill said.

'What's not a priority around here?' Choi sat back in her chair and put her feet up on her desk.

Jill shrugged. 'I've been trying to bring myself up to speed on the Red Cave Gang. I read high school students are being recruited by friends and branded with a gang tattoo on their stomachs to mark their initiation.'

'Yeah, and it isn't just Asian kids anymore, they're recruiting across cultures.' Choi reached into her pocket and threw her phone on her desk. 'Overtime's been approved, so expect to work extra hours on this one. The leader is a guy called Vincent Wan. He's a slimy bastard and the sooner he's deported the better.' Choi grabbed a bottle of water from her desk drawer. 'He's into everything: drug distribution, extortion, kidnapping, identity theft, and child prostitution. You name it;

he's got a finger in it. He needs to be put on a slow boat back to Malaysia, preferably one with holes in it.'

'Definitely one to get off the streets.'

Choi nodded but then leaned forward. 'I'm sorry about what happened to Robbie Calloway. I heard you two used to be an item.'

Who didn't know about her and Robbie? 'Yeah, we went out for a while.'

'Did you know he had gambling debts?' Choi asked.

Jill raised her eyes. 'We were close, but not close enough for him to discuss his financial situation with me.' Jill rested her eyes on Jenny Choi. 'How do you know about his gambling?'

'I had a call this morning from a DS I know. We were talking about Robbie. He told me he'd bumped into him at Randwick racetrack a few months back. Robbie was laying down some pretty serious bets, boasting to him about how much he'd won.' Choi dropped her feet to the floor. She unscrewed the cap of the bottled water and took a swig. 'I figured if he'd won money, he must have lost some as well, so I asked around. One of my sources told me he owed money to Billy Veland.'

'Veland's got some pretty unpleasant types working for him, hasn't he?' Jill asked.

'Yeah, but he's small time, mostly lends money for credit card and mortgage payments.'

'Still…definitely worth a follow up. So, where do I find him?'

'He's got a shoe repair shop in one of the arcades in Lane Cove. He's a short, surly type.'

The case may be closed as far as Rimis was concerned, but Jill still had questions that needed answers.

# THIRTEEN

JILL AND JENNY CHOI WALKED through the automatic glass doors of North Shore Hospital. The foyer resembled a lounge at a busy international airport with rows of flower stalls, gift shops and comfortable lounges. The aroma of fresh coffee masked the smell of cleaning agents and antiseptic.

'I could do with a coffee,' Choi said.

'I hate hospitals, the less time we spend here the better.' Jill shuddered. 'You don't mind, do you?'

'No worries, I can wait until we get back to Chatswood.' Hospitals held too many memories for Jill, especially North Shore Hospital. Memories of her father as he lay in the intensive care, memories of herself as a patient here after Kevin Taggart had attacked her in her apartment.

Jill and Choi joined a line of visitors and queued for the lifts. While they waited, Jill thought about Adam Lee and why she'd joined the force. She'd thought she'd be able to protect someone like Adam but she'd been fooling herself. In all the years she'd been a police officer there had never been a single person whose life she'd been able to change. The ping of the open lift caught her attention and brought her back to the moment. She jostled for a space next to the lift door and pressed the button to level fourteen.

Jill followed Choi out of the lift and past the nurse's station to Adam Lee's private room. Choi knocked on the door. They walked in to see him propped up against a pile of pillows, the television set on and a tray stacked with uneaten food at his bedside. The file said Adam Lee was nineteen but he looked more like sixteen with his baby-face and high cheek-bones. His eyes were dark and his black hair was cropped close and fashionably styled.

Adam Lee turned his eyes away from the television and looked at them. 'How are you Adam? You're looking much better than the last time I saw you,' Choi said. 'I see you've still got the tubes in.'

'Yeah. But they said I could be going home in a few days.' Adam looked at Jill.

'This is Detective Jill Brennan,' Choi said. 'She's working with me on your case.'

Jill smiled. She wanted to put him at ease so he'd open up to her. 'You'll be pleased to be going home, then.' Jill pulled up a visitor chair and sat down beside him.

On the surface at least, Adam looked like he'd made a good recovery.

Uniform had been conducting extra patrols at the Interchange and they appeared to be effective because there hadn't been any similar incidents reported.

'Adam,' Jill said, 'given you're about to leave hospital it's even more important you tell us who attacked you. If the person who did this to you goes unpunished, there's a good chance he'll attack again. You may even be targeted. You might not be so lucky next time.' She leaned forward. 'Instead of a collapsed lung it could be something worse.'

He gave a shrug, turned up the TV.

Jill wasn't going to be put off that easily. 'Or maybe they'll go after your family.'

He gave her a glance at that one.

Jill continued. 'When Detective Choi came to speak to you last time, you said you didn't know who attacked you or anything about an organisation called the Red Cave Gang. I'm sorry, Adam but I don't believe you. It's important you tell us the name of the person who stabbed you so we can question him. And hopefully, if he's part of this gang, we'll be able to put a stop to their operation.'

'Okay, okay. Give me a break.' He lowered his voice. 'I don't know about any gang, but the dude who did this to me was Benny Cheung. His old man was an eye doctor. Had a shop on Victoria Road next to the disposal store.'

Cheung. Jill recognised that name. The guy found in the boot of his car. 'So, tell me, what happened?' Jill leaned forward. She had a pen and her notebook in her hand.

'I was minding my own business. I'd just got off the train. I'd been in the city with some mates and I was walking back to my old man's restaurant when he attacked me, right out of the blue. He pulled a knife on me then took off after he stabbed me.'

'You told Detective Choi you had no idea why he pulled a knife on you. Is that still the case?'

Adam shrugged. 'He just went crazy.'

Jill knew it was Adam Lee's word against Benjamin Cheung's. The CCTV camera where the attack occurred had been smashed the day before and hadn't been replaced. Unfortunate or convenient for Lee? She also wondered why Adam was now prepared to talk and why he'd referred to David Cheung in the past tense. What had the Cheung family been involved in? Were they members of the Red Cave Gang? Whether they were or not, it didn't matter now. The father was dead and his wife and Benjamin were missing. She grabbed the remote control for the television and turned it off.

'Hey, I was watching that.'

'I need your full attention here, Adam.' She put the remote down on his bedside table.

'Did anyone see Benjamin Cheung attack you?'

'Nope.'

'So, nobody came to your aid?'

'It was late, the mall was deserted.'

If there had been any witnesses Jill wondered if they'd come forward. If the attack on Adam had anything to do with the Red Cave Gang, any witnesses would've been warned off. 'Thanks for co-operating, Adam.' Jill handed him back the remote control. 'We might be back with more questions, if that's all right.'

'Yeah, no worries, I'm not goin' anywhere.' Adam turned the television back on.

Jill and Choi left the room and took the lift down to the lobby.

'I've got a feeling he wasn't being totally honest with us. What do you think?'

'I agree but at least he gave us a name,' Choi said. 'And a very interesting one at that.'

'I'm a bit suspicious though. Why is he speaking to us now? What's changed?'

Jill shrugged. 'Maybe someone convinced him to offer up Benjamin Cheung's name.'

# FOURTEEN

JILL AND FIN WERE ON their way to the morgue. At least Fin had made some effort. She'd showered, her hair was washed and she was dressed in a pair of denim jeans, a pale blue shirt and a black knee-length coat. She'd even managed to cover the smell of booze. Mints and perfume were working overtime.

It was normally a ten-minute drive to the morgue but the tail end of the peak-hour traffic made for slow going — not helped by the rain. Jill kept the headlights on and the wipers turned to intermittent. It would have been smarter if she'd taken the back streets instead of busy Parramatta Road. She backtracked, turned right at Barr Street and a few minutes later pulled into the car park at the rear of the Glebe Morgue.

Jill walked with Fin along the building's corridors, which smelled of formaldehyde and air freshener. When they reached the viewing room, Jill pushed open the door and they walked in. Jill had stood in this room with its dusty plastic flowers and tissue boxes more times than she would like to remember. An on-call counsellor who was in the room had her head bowed, respecting the formalities. Words of comfort and commiseration would be offered after Fin ID'ed Robbie.

'Fin, is this Robert Calloway, your brother?'

Fin nodded and held her hands to her face. 'Yes, oh my God.' Fin slumped into Jill's arms.

'How about we have a cup of tea?' the counsellor said. 'We can go into my office and deal with the paperwork there.'

'We just need you to sign a form,' Jill said to Fin. As if grief wasn't enough, there were also the rituals of death to be performed: decisions to be made, funeral arrangements, Robbie's estate.

Eventually, Jill managed to get Fin out of the morgue and into her detective's car. It was raining when they arrived at Fin's apartment. Jill buttoned her coat. 'I'll walk you up.'

Fin fumbled with her house keys. Jill gently took them from her and opened the door.

'Is there anyone I can call to be with you, Fin? You shouldn't be alone.' Jill remembered similar words spoken by Rimis the night Robbie died.

Fin didn't answer immediately. She wiped her nose with a crumpled tissue and collapsed onto the sofa. 'There's no one. The doctor came last night. He gave me tablets to help me sleep. I think I'll take one.'

Jill reached into her coat pocket and pulled out a card. She wrote down her private mobile number. 'Here, take this. You can call me 24/7. I'll always answer it. I'm here for you, Fin.'


Jill returned to the station and drove into the basement car park. She switched off the engine and let her head sink onto the steering wheel. The police radio crackled in the background.

Mental images of Robbie came to her. Robbie at the beach with his surfboard, zinc cream on his nose. Robbie in his police uniform, tall and straight. His cheeky grin. Robbie propped up at the bar of the pub they used to frequent. Robbie in a body bag at the base of the clock tower.

Jill went over the last time she'd seen Robbie. New Year's Day. Jazz playing in the background, leftover tinsel and gaudy lights from Christmas still hanging above the bar. Robbie had spoken to her about his future and the plans he had to keep rising up the ranks. They'd joked that one day she'd be reporting to him.

In that last phone call, had he been reaching out to her? She'd never know. She slammed her fist against the steering wheel, and then gripped the wheel, tight, with both hands. A few seconds later tears streamed down her face, the sobs coming hard and fast.

# FIFTEEN

FROM THE WINDOW IN HIS office, all Rimis could see on Archer Street were the tops of umbrellas. Buses rumbled by, splashing up water from the gutters. When the call had come through on Friday night he was told the body of a police officer had been found at Callan Park. He had no idea Brennan knew Robbie Calloway. He ran his hand through his hair. Choi had said Brennan seemed tired and that maybe she needed time off. Knowing Brennan she wouldn't be sleeping because of the events of the last two days. He wasn't surprised. She reminded him of what he was like when he first got his detective's designation. She was bull-headed, tenacious and just as much a pain in the arse as he'd been — perhaps, still was.

Robbie Calloway's death was an open-and-shut case even though the autopsy hadn't been done. Calloway had landed feet first, he had a gambling problem, had visited mental health sites and his home reflected a man in trouble. Soon the file would be archived. Brennan was far from convinced Calloway had taken his own life but he hoped for her sake she'd accept his death and move on. If she continued to pursue the case and go against orders, it could affect her career.

Still, it was interesting that Scott Carver had reservations too.

There was a knock on the door. He turned around. Brennan. He knew she'd been to the morgue with Fin Calloway. 'How are you holding up?'

'I'm okay, but I can't say the same for Fin Calloway.'

'Sure you don't want time off?' Rimis asked.

'No need for that.'

Rimis nodded. It probably wouldn't be the last time he made that offer. He walked back to his desk and told her to take a seat.

Jill leaned over and handed him an A4 envelope. 'Here are the photos from the CCTV cameras at Callan Park.'

He flicked through the photos. 'This is all you've got? What about footage from the cameras in the courtyard?'

'They weren't operational,' Jill said. 'And there are no other cameras apart from the one in the car park.'

Rimis rolled his eyes and slid the photos back across the desk to Jill. 'You better give Scott Carver a call and tell him the CCTV was a waste of time.'

He couldn't believe the lack of security in Callan Park. It was different when he started his career, all you had to rely on were witnesses, but over the past decade, Sydney had become a city of cameras — public and private. Policing had changed with the technology, now it was standard procedure to look for cameras at every crime scene.

'There's not much to work with,' Jill said. 'The security company tried to enhance the tape but it's low-grade, and there's not much of it because of the camera angle. Hard to tell, but it could have been Robbie based on the frame and height. And the rain jacket looks like the one Patullo found in Robbie's backpack. When I was in Fin's apartment, I noticed she had one exactly the same.' Jill flipped the pages of her notebook. 'The next movement was Patrick Hill's dog running across the car park. That was at 10.36 pm. Eight minutes later, Mr Hill appeared. It matches his story. Patullo and his partner arrived at 11.02.' Jill snapped her notebook shut. 'That's it. No one else, not surprising. It was a god-awful night to be out.'

Rimis leaned forward and looked at the photos again. 'It could be Robbie Calloway or any number of people. Navy blue rain jackets are a dime a dozen. You said yourself Fin had a rain jacket just like it. Christ, even I've got one.' He leaned back. Sighed. 'Look, Brennan, I think you need to drop this. You're letting your imagination and your feelings run away with you. Besides, we don't have the resources or the manpower to have you running around looking for evidence of foul play when there clearly is none. You know we've got a backlog of cases that need our attention.' Rimis didn't think she was listening.

'There's another way of getting to the tower without being seen,' Jill said. 'Someone could have approached from the east, along Kirkbride Way and —'

'You're clutching at straws, now.'

Jill glared at him. 'We're still waiting for the autopsy results.' He paused. 'You need to let it go.'

'But —'

'I said, let it go.' Rimis pushed his empty coffee cup to the side of his desk to make a point. Then, he looked at her. 'What do you expect the tox reports will tell you, anyway? Even if they show alcohol or drugs in his blood, it doesn't mean a damn thing. In fact, it will prove the opposite and support the theory he jumped, or fell from the tower while under the influence.'

'But —'

Rimis shot to his feet. He had to be firm with her…it was the only thing she'd respond to. 'I mean what I say, Jill. Leave it alone, the less attention drawn to Robbie Calloway's suicide, the better. You have to learn when to obey orders. I've covered for you before, but this time powerful people are involved, the type of people who wouldn't think twice about kicking your arse from here to kingdom come.'

'What do you mean powerful people?'

'For starters, the Police Commissioner and then there's the Premier. It seems Katrina Andrel has a bee in her bonnet about their failure to act on the increase in suicides in the emergency services over the past twelve months. Nobody, wants to dwell on what's seen in the press as our failures…failure to protect one of our own.' Rimis sighed and ran his hand across the back of his neck. 'Listen, Jill, we've got more pressing things on our plate at the moment. Real criminals. Remember them? I want to know if Asian gangs are involved in the Adam Lee knife attack and David Cheung's murder.'

# SIXTEEN

THE WIND PICKED UP. Rimis gripped his coat closed with one hand and darted across the road to the Great Northern Hotel on the corner of Mowbray Road. He would have preferred to meet DCI Scott Carver at Otto's Bar, but it was on the other side of town and he had a pile of paperwork waiting for him back on his desk.

The hotel's wood-panelled interior, antique Chesterfield lounges and faux deer head, reminded him of an old English hunting lodge. He spotted Carver sitting at a table next to the open fire, studying the lunch menu.

There were advantages to being a DI, Rimis thought as he stopped at the bar but he thought he'd be pushing his luck if he ordered a glass of red, so he ordered tomato juice instead. When his drink arrived he went over to join Chief Inspector Carver.

Carver stood up. 'Good to see you again, Nick.' They shook hands.

'Good to see you too, Scotty. It's blowing a gale out there.' Rimis put his glass down on the table and draped his coat over the back of the chair. He glanced up at the flat-screen television mounted on the wall. The soccer was on and Argentina was playing Uruguay. The volume was turned down low. He picked up the menu and gave it a momentary glance.

'Still playing golf?' Rimis asked.

'Yeah, I've been working on my handicap. Takes time, lots of practice, like anything else.' Carver looked down at his glass. 'I was having a look at last quarter's crime stats before I left the office. North Shore Local Area Command figures are looking good…there's been a drop in break and enters.'

'We do our best. Community policing seems to be working. Detective Choi, our local liaison officer, does a good job interfacing with the Chinese community.'

'Yes. Detective Jenny Choi. I read her report on Adam Lee, the Asian boy who was attacked at the Interchange. I still think the assault on Lee has something to do with these Asian gangs operating all over Sydney. That attack last week on the restaurant in Dixon Street, we're pretty certain was part of Red Cave's bid to extend its control from Hurstville and Parramatta to Chinatown.

They could be pushing for control in Chatswood as well. Keep me informed, will you? We've got to put a stop to these gangs before we lose control. Up until now they only targeted the Asian community for its membership, but now they're recruiting along social rather than ethnic lines.' Carver took a sip of his water. 'And what about this optometrist who was murdered, David Cheung?'

'I've got Detectives Brennan and Rawlings working on the case.' Rimis pulled at his tie. 'We established Mrs Cheung and their son, Benjamin, boarded a flight to Hong Kong the night Cheung was murdered. If we can track them down, they might be able to shed some light.' Rimis eyed Carver, sensed he wanted to talk to him about something other than crime statistics and Asian gangs. The conversation to date was a phone call, not a lunch meeting.

'What do you feel like to eat? I normally have the fish and chips, they're always good,' Rimis said.

'Okay then, I'll have the same. Order some extra lemon with it, will you?'

Rimis ordered the two meals and returned with a set of cutlery and napkins.

Scott fiddled with his knife. 'Terrible business, this suicide at Callan Park.'

Ah, so that was it.

'How's morale?' Carver asked.

'Not good.'

Carver nodded.

Rimis glanced up at the screen. Argentina had just scored a goal. 'We checked Calloway's computer. He'd visited a couple of mental health sites and when I spoke to his boss, DI Perris, he told me Calloway had used up all his annual leave and sick leave. Also said he'd seen a change in his attitude recently.' Rimis took a sip from his glass. 'There's talk he had a gambling problem.'

Carver raised his eyebrows.

'Horses,' Rimis said. 'Perris was planning to have a disciplinary talk with him, but never got the chance.'

'What about drugs and alcohol? Usually if you're addicted to one, you're addicted to the other.'

'We're still waiting on the autopsy,' Rimis said.

Scott Carver moved the salt and pepper, shakers to the middle of the table. 'What's your opinion of Jill Brennan?' Carver asked.

'Jill?' Rimis smiled. 'She can be a loose cannon at times but she's one of the best officers I've ever worked with. She's hard-working, intelligent, dedicated, and possesses an inherent tendency to follow her instincts.'

Carver leaned back in his chair, crossed his arms. 'Her father was the same. Mickey was always going out on a limb to get a result, and look what happened to him.'

Rimis didn't need to be reminded of what happened to Mickey Brennan. The man behind the Kevin Taggart art fraud case was Dorin Chisca, a Romanian drug lord who gunned down Jill's father in a drug raid in Lakemba.

Rimis rubbed his chin and remembered how he'd taken Brennan to task about the way the Taggart case had ended, but he'd also praised her for her cool head when the crazy mongrel turned up at her apartment with murder on his mind.

'Scotty, there's something I think you need to know.'

'Go on,' Carver said.

'Calloway's gun's missing. We've searched his house, but there's no sign of it.' Carver was silent for a bit, then: 'I might as well be frank with you, Nick. I did have my doubts at first, but the more I hear about what was going on in Calloway's life, the more I'm convinced it was suicide. And now his gun? Maybe he had plans to use it on himself, chickened out at the last moment and jumped from the tower, instead.'

'Yeah, that's what I was thinking. But that doesn't explain where the gun is. Either way, we need to find it.'

Scott Carver nodded. 'I agree.'

They talked about golf and Rimis's gym class he'd signed up for until their meals arrived.

'Fish and chips?'

Both Carver and Rimis looked up at the attractive waitress. She smiled and put the plates down in front of them.

Rimis squeezed tomato sauce over his chips. Carver squeezed lemon on his fish. They ate in silence for a few minutes, before Carver spoke between mouthfuls.

'Look, Nick, as you know Calloway's death has wider repercussions. And everyone knows politically, Callan Park is a no-go zone.' Carver put down his knife and fork and wiped his mouth with a paper napkin. 'The less attention drawn to it, the better. And the Commissioner is none too happy with the effect Calloway's suicide is having on morale.' Carver took a few more bites. 'The media and the police association are up in arms over it as well; they're calling for more support for police officers living with PTSD. Did you watch that documentary last night on SBS?'

'Yeah, couldn't believe the timing.' Rimis knew frontline policing was one of the most difficult and selfless jobs in society. Just by doing their job, police officers faced as much emotional trauma as military personnel serving inside a war zone. But nobody within the force wanted to talk about Post Traumatic Stress Disorder. It was considered a contagious disease; show empathy to colleagues, you become weak and end up in a downward spiral yourself.

They finished their meals in silence.

When he was done, Carver pushed his empty plate to one side. 'There've been mumblings from above, Nick. When mental health and Callan Park are mentioned in the same sentence, there's always a political backlash. Nobody wants to have a cop suicide rubbed in their faces, nor do they want a reminder of Callan Park's dark past as a lunatic asylum.'

Rimis sighed. It was a no-go zone, all right. Now he just had to convince Jill.

# SEVENTEEN

THE TRAFFIC WAS LIGHT AND if it stayed that way Jill would be home in time to have a quick shower before she met up with Bea and Harry for dinner. Bea had made the booking at Mojo's over two weeks ago and even though she didn't feel like going out tonight, dinner with Bea and Harry was exactly what she needed to help take her mind off Robbie.

She was hoping it wouldn't be a late night, because Rimis had told her before she'd left the station that Scott Carver wanted to see her at Parramatta at 8 am tomorrow morning. He hadn't said what it was about.

Jill managed to score a park right outside her apartment block. The apartment didn't come with a car space and given the popularity of New South Head Road, she rarely got a park in front of the building.

She stopped by the bank of letterboxes to collect her mail before she took the stairs to the second floor and let herself into her apartment. After she closed the door, she turned the dead bolt, pressed the button lock, and fastened the security chain. Before Kevin Taggart, her personal safety wasn't something she'd thought much about. Now, she was compelled to surround herself with it, a natural response to being violated in her own home.

Once she'd put her mail on the sideboard next to the framed photo of her parents on their wedding day, she headed for the bathroom. She locked the door, undressed, stepped into the shower and turned the taps on full. The hot water assaulted her body but it didn't help ease the numbness she felt.

Forty minutes later, Jill entered Mojo's Tapas Bar on Campbell Parade. She spotted Bea and Harry at a corner table. At the table next to them, a group of four couples was making a commotion over the seating arrangements.

Jill loved everything Spanish — the food, the language, the culture, and the music. Her mother was Spanish and Jill had often thought it strange she'd given her an Irish name rather than a Spanish one. Something like Juanita or Josefina appealed to Jill far more than Jillian. Then again, despite her Spanish heritage, with her blonde hair and peaches-and-cream complexion, she was pure Irish.

The Spanish lessons she'd taken after she left university were part of her plan to travel to Spain. She hoped to track down her mother's family. Make some connection. She knew her mother had a sister but her father had never spoken about her. Jill had a feeling there'd been a family falling out when her mother left for Australia.

Jill waved to Harry and Bea. At the table, Bea stood and hugged her and then Harry pulled out a chair and kissed her on both cheeks.

'Rough day?' he asked.

'Yeah.' She didn't have to say anything more, her face told the story.

'Harry and I were so upset when we heard about Robbie.' Bea grabbed Jill's hands in hers. 'And every time I call you, your phone goes to voicemail.'

'I'm sorry, Bea. It's been crazy lately, and it's hard to find the time to answer personal calls.'

Bea squeezed Jill's hands. 'I'm just glad you remembered dinner tonight.

So we could talk.'

Harry filled Jill's glass with Sangria.

'We saw that documentary on Post Traumatic Stress Disorder on SBS last night.' Bea leaned in closer to Jill. 'You'd tell us if you were having problems coping with the job, wouldn't you?'

'Of course. And I'm fine. Seriously.'

'When did you last see Robbie?' Harry asked.

Strange you should ask, Harry. I saw him this morning at the morgue. Jill swallowed hard. 'We caught up on New Year's Day. He seemed okay, great even. He'd been promoted. He seemed happy enough with his life.' Jill sipped her sangria. 'He was drunk of course. Showing off, you know what he was like. But he didn't give me any reason to think anything was wrong.' Jill shook her head. 'I guess a lot can happen in six months.' She drained her glass.

'Was he in some sort of trouble?' Harry asked. 'People don't usually take their own life unless something's worrying them. Was he gambling again?'

'I think so.'

'Maybe he got in over his head,' Harry said. 'And he couldn't see a way out of it.'

'And sometimes people kill themselves for no apparent reason,' Bea added. 'A daughter of one of my clients took an overdose — she'd just got a place at university. The poor girl had her whole life ahead of her.'

Jill watched Harry's steady hand refill her glass. If she drank too much tonight, she knew he'd drive her home and she could pick her car up in the morning. She was rostered on for an eight-hour shift and she didn't have to start until nine. Although first up was that meeting with Scott Carver, and she certainly couldn't turn up to that with a hangover. Normally, she worked twelve-hour shifts, 6 am to 6 pm, plus two day shifts and two nights a week but because of the increase in their caseload she'd volunteered to work extra shifts.

'Last week Robbie left a message on my voicemail. I forgot to call him back. Forgot,' she whispered. 'I can't stop thinking I could have done something. I wish I knew what he'd wanted to talk to me about.'

'It's not your fault, Jill. You can't blame yourself. It was Robbie's decision to take his life,' Harry said.

Jill paused. 'That's the thing, Harry. I don't think it was suicide.' Harry and Bea looked at her. 'What do you mean?' Bea asked.

'I can't see Robbie taking his own life. Can you? He'd moved from Collaroy to Callan Park two weeks ago. Why would he do that? And why Rozelle of all places, and across the road from Callan Park?'

The next table was in full swing. Bea moved her chair closer to Jill and put her arm around her shoulders. Jill propped her elbows on the table, rubbed her hands over her face. 'I know, what you're thinking Bea. It's written all over your face. You think I'm in denial, don't you?'

'I think you haven't allowed yourself to grieve.' Bea took Jill's hand. 'You know you can always talk to me, anytime, day or night.'

'I know, Bea. Thanks.' Jill could always count on Bea, their friendship was something they both took seriously. She picked up her glass and sipped the sangria again. 'I'm just a bit raw at the moment.'

She had to find out what had been going on in Robbie's life since she saw him last. She was sure he would have told her if there was something bothering him. Was that why he'd called? Even Fin had realised something was up with Robbie.

Jill pulled back on her ponytail and picked up her menu.

'I played golf with Scott Carver last weekend,' Harry said. He looked over the top of his menu. 'He was asking after you.'

'Was he now.' Scott Carver. As if she didn't have enough on her mind. She took a deep breath to compose herself. 'Now, let's order.' For the first time in days Jill had an appetite. 'I don't know what you're having, but I think the calamari with citrus sauce looks good.'

# EIGHTEEN

JILL WOKE IN A POOL of sweat. The bed sheets were wet, her mouth dry. Her heart pounded and her chest heaved as she took in deep, jagged breaths to calm herself. She turned on the bedside lamp and stared up at the ceiling. It was always the same theme — death — but with different scenarios. Sometimes she was struggling to keep Kevin Taggart at bay, her strength spent, his foul breath on her face, and the crush of his weight on her. Other times her father featured, his death raw, like it had happened days ago not years. Dorin Chisca, the man responsible for his death, waving a gun in her face, mocking her.

It wasn't quite daybreak but Jill knew from experience, the chance of further sleep was impossible. She slipped out of bed, pulled the quilt around her shoulders and walked out of the bedroom into the kitchen. She turned on the light above the range hood and poured herself a glass of water. Too tired to think, too wound up to sleep, she stood in front of the window, stretched over and checked the lock. Everything was secure. She yawned, knew if she didn't get at least seven uninterrupted hours of decent sleep sometime soon, she was going to start making mistakes, and mistakes were something she couldn't afford in her line of work.

Outside, a branch scraped against the glass. She jumped back with a start. With all the memories in the apartment, why hadn't she left, moved somewhere else? She frowned, bit down on a nail. Kevin Taggart. Stop thinking about him, you know he can't hurt you any-more.

Jill swallowed her water in a gulp, put the glass down and turned her thoughts to Robbie. It wouldn't be long before the case would be formally closed. Then all that remained would be to go to Robbie's funeral.

Jill showered, towelled herself off and brushed her hair back into the usual ponytail. She'd decided to wear make-up today. She dabbed on some lipstick and applied tinted moisturiser. She searched everywhere for the black A-line skirt that had been missing for the past month. Eventually she found it at the bottom of her wardrobe. The skirt was the only one she owned. She usually felt more comfortable in jeans or slacks, but today she needed a look that said power and authority. She teamed the outfit with a black jacket and a dusty-pink, silk blouse.

Too bad the whole effect required heels; by the end of the day her feet would be hot and swollen. Jill finally found her black stilettos under the bed. The shoes had been bought on sale, and on impulse, but she knew the heels would give her the height she needed to look Carver in the eye.

She walked into the kitchen and popped two slices of wholegrain bread into the toaster. She would have preferred a later meeting time to avoid the peak-hour traffic. What was this meeting with Scott Carver about, anyway? She bit into a slice of toast and wondered if he wanted to talk to her about Adam Lee and the Inter-change. She knew nothing about Asian gangs. That was Jenny Choi's area.

# NINETEEN

THE TRAFFIC ON NEW SOUTH Head Road was slow but at least it was moving. Jill checked the time on the dashboard. It was almost two and half kilometres to the Cross City Tunnel. Why was she driving all the way out to Parramatta? Whatever Scott Carver had to say to her, surely it could have been said in an email or over the phone.

Jill had first met Chief Inspector Carver at Bea and Harry's son's first birthday party around the time of the undercover assignment into art fraud. They'd been the only single people there — the other guests were all married with kids. She loved Bea like a sister but she was always trying to set Jill up with every eligible man she came across. If she liked them, she assumed Jill would too.

At the party, he'd introduced himself as Scott, Harry's golfing partner. Bea had finally got it right. She'd saved the best for last. Scott was good-looking, well-educated and the fact he was far too good to be true should have rung warning bells. She shuddered when she remembered the embarrassment she'd felt shortly afterwards when she had gone with Rimis to a meeting at Police Headquarters. She had no idea the Scott she'd met at Bea's party was Scott Carver, the Area Commander of North West Area Command.

Jill jumped at the sound of a horn from the car behind. The traffic light had turned green. Jill raised her hand in apology and put her foot on the accelerator.

After she'd broken up with Robbie she'd decided never to date cops… never, ever. The decision had left her chances of finding a partner slim. As for long-term relationships, she could count those on one hand. She remembered what Jenny Choi had said to her on her first day at Chatswood. Rule number one; don't screw the crew. Rule number two; never let a man become indispensable. The last man that had come close to meaning anything to her was William Phillips, who was almost old enough to be her father. To complicate matters she'd met him on one of the worst days of his life — Jill had been the officer assigned to tell Phillips his mother was dead. There had been a time during their short relationship she'd thought it might work, but in the end he couldn't handle the demands of her job.

When Jill arrived at Police Headquarters in Parramatta she was told Chief Inspector Carver was in a meeting. Jill settled back in the visitor chair and flicked through her emails. Ten minutes later she heard a phone ring.

'Detective Brennan?' Jill looked up.

'Chief Inspector Carver, will see you now.'

Jill walked into Scott Carver's plush office. He stood up and walked out from behind his desk. He was wearing a tailored suit; a crisp white shirt matched with a pale grey tie. 'Sorry I kept you waiting, Jill. Come in.' Carver closed the door and pulled a leather visitor chair out for her. Jill sat down and hoped he didn't notice the deep breath she took before she crossed her legs. Wisps of her honey-blonde hair escaped her ponytail. She brushed them behind her ear. Scott Carver perched himself on the corner of his desk next to her.

Bea had never told her how old Scott Carver was; late thirties, early forties, she guessed. He had a few character lines around his eyes and grey hairs around his temples, which made him look distinguished in a sexy sort of way. As he talked, she detected the subtle scent of his woody aftershave, noticed the way his thigh muscles flexed through his trousers when he moved his leg. Jill tried to concentrate on what he was saying; aware of the effect he was having on her.

Talk turned to Bea and Harry and their son. When coffee was offered it was declined and then they got down to why she was in his office. They went over what Jill knew about Adam Lee and he told her their Intel suggested there was more to the attack than a case of assault but he wasn't at liberty to disclose any details. He then went on to fill her in on the Asian Gang strike force. Officers from Chatswood, Hurstville, Strathfield and Cabramatta Local Area Commands were being recruited.

'I want you to put all your other cases aside and concentrate on Adam Lee. I've already spoken to DI Rimis and we've agreed that you and Detective Choi would be the perfect pair from our region to work on this. I'm not sure how much you know, but Vincent Wan is the leader of the Red Cave Gang. He's a Chinese-Malaysian national. Immigration is going to deport him if we ever find him. He's a stand-over merchant and ICAC also have him and a few of his associates in their sights.'

'Can I ask why you think Adam Lee is associated with the Red Cave Gang?' Jill asked.

'Recent Intel suggests Wan's operation is based in Chatswood but we don't know where exactly. There's a lot of ground to cover and the local community isn't exactly forthcoming.'

'And, Adam Lee? What is it you want Jenny Choi and me to do?'

'I want you to gain his trust. He might lead us to Vincent Wan.' Carver straightened the creases on his trousers. 'Jill, there was something else I wanted to talk to you about.'

Jill felt the chemistry between them, wondered if Scott Carver felt it too. 'I know you have your doubts about Robbie Calloway's death but…'

The look he gave her told her she was on dangerous ground.

Jill straightened her back. 'I knew Robbie well and I'm still not convinced he took his own life.' She thought she was here to talk about Adam Lee and Asian Gangs, not Robbie.

'Surely with everything going on in his life it would be enough to convince you he committed suicide. It convinced me. So what have I missed?'

'Fin. Robbie was devoted to his sister. I can't imagine he'd leave her alone intentionally, and if he had taken his own life, at the very least he would have left Fin a note.' Jill purposively didn't mention that even that close bond had drifted in the few months before his death.

'Any idea why he relocated to Rozelle just two weeks before his death?' Carver asked.

'No. Work seems the most likely though. I'm sure you're aware of Robbie's reputation for taking all of his cases seriously. His promotion to Senior Constable after he got a result with that sex offender in Palm Beach is proof of how committed he was to the job.'

Jill could see Scott Carver thinking. She wanted to convince him Robbie's death was worthy of further investigation. She continued. 'Maybe he found something he didn't have time to share with the other members of his team. And if he had discovered something, whatever it was may have led him to Glover Street, and ultimately to his death.'

'Come on Jill, that's pure speculation. You're aware he visited mental help sites?'

'That could have been because he was trying to find help for his sister. She doesn't seem well.'

'She just lost her brother. Of course she's not well.'

Jill ran her hands down her skirt. 'Even if Robbie visited those sites because of his state of mind, it was a positive thing, don't you think? It means he was looking for answers. And the lack of a suicide note, surely that's an important factor.'

Scott's eyebrows twitched in surprise. 'Not everyone who commits suicide leaves a note. You know that as well as I do.' Carver's tone was light but Jill also detected a hint of impatience. It seemed like the ranks were closing in on her.

Why was everyone so eager to accept Robbie had taken his own life? Robbie Calloway was a long-serving officer. He deserved more. And why did she get the feeling that there was something more than polite interest behind Scott Carver's questions?

'Did you know Robbie well?' she asked.

Scott shrugged. 'He's within my command.' He cleared his throat. 'We had a couple of beers on a few occasions.' Scott stood and changed the topic. 'What about his gun? I believe it's missing and it looks like he took it home without proper authorisation the night before he died.'

Jill nodded. 'That's right. Someone saw him put it into his backpack.' She knew what Scott was thinking, that Robbie had taken his gun home to use on himself.

Carver walked over to the window, turned around to face her. 'Did you know he took out a life insurance policy last month?'

'No, I didn't.' Jill tried to hide her surprise. It seemed like Scott Carver had been doing his own investigating.

Scott crossed the room. 'Look, how about we go downstairs and grab a coffee?'

Jill stood up. He was close. He paused, eyes on her. She shuddered, imagining his hands on her. Another pause and she wondered if he was feeling as conflicted as she was. Wanting to kiss him, touch him, but too worried about the consequences. She was about to take a step back, snap to her senses when his hand touched her face, stroked her hair. In the end it was Scott who closed the distance and pressed his lips against hers. She kissed him back, caught up in the moment. But she had to break the spell. This was work, and he was an area commander, for God's sake.

She gently pushed him away. 'Don't,' she said. Her face reddened and desire welled up inside her. 'This isn't a good idea. In fact this is a terrible idea.' She took a step back. 'And besides, there's no point.'

He searched her face. 'What do you mean?'

'You and me, it's never going to work.'

'Why? I thought it was working just fine.' He raised his eyebrows, referring to the kiss.

'It's not that, it's just —'

'I haven't stopped thinking about you since I met you at Harry and Bea's. I was surprised you didn't return my phone calls,' Carver said.

'I'm sorry. There was so much happening back then. The Taggart case threw me. It was…' she gripped the top of the chair, 'tough.'

'And that's why I called you again when I heard Taggart had tried to —'

'Thanks. And I'm sorry I never called you back.' She took a breath. 'But it wasn't just that. I don't date cops.'

'A wise policy. I can see the sense in not letting the people you work with see you naked.' Scott's tone was light but his eyes were saying something else all together.

'I mean it, Scott. Look at us. What do you see?'

'Two people strongly attracted to each other.' His eyes met hers.

'Apart from that.' She crossed her arms. 'You know what I see? Two over-worked cops.'

'I'm not asking you to marry me, Jill. I just thought we could go out together, have a bit of fun.'

'Even fun can be hard in the workplace,' Jill said, slightly nauseated by the prospect that he might only be interested in a fling. What did she really know about him? Maybe he routinely slept with his female colleagues. 'Besides, now is really not a good time.'

'In our line of work is there ever a good time?' Carver threw his shoulders back. 'I apologise. I guess I misjudged the body language and what was going on here.' Scott's eyes were coolly disapproving as they met hers. 'You know something? I don't think it has anything to do with timing or being a cop. I think you use the fact you're a cop to stop you from forming relationships.'

Jill's cheeks turned a vibrant shade of red. She turned to leave but Scott seized her arm.

'I know you're upset over Calloway's death because of your…history with him. Perhaps that's why you're seeing his death as something more sinister.'

The hide of him. Did he really think her judgement was clouded because she'd slept with Robbie? She was about to tell him to mind his own business, but thought better of it and bit her tongue. After all he was an area commander.

Carver sighed and let go of her. 'We'll probably never know what he was doing at Callan Park last Friday night. You can't always expect an explanation for everything that happens in our business. Chances are he was out for a walk, saw the tower and...' He trailed off. 'Or maybe he went to Callan Park for one reason and one reason only: to kill himself.'

# TWENTY

JILL DIDN'T DRIVE STRAIGHT BACK to the station after her meeting with Scott Carver; instead, she took the Ryde exit off the motorway to Lane Cove. If Scott Carver and Nick Rimis thought she'd walk away before she fully investigated Robbie's death, they were both mistaken. There was one thing at least in Scott Carver's favour. He hadn't immediately written Robbie's death off as suicide like everyone else. But just because he'd eventually accepted the suicide explanation didn't mean Jill had to, and after this morning's meeting she was more determined than ever to discover the truth behind Robbie's death.

After driving around in circles for almost ten minutes, Jill finally found a parking space in the Woolworths basement car park in Lane Cove. She locked the car and took the escalators up to Longueville Road.

Her pace was hurried and she was aware of the clicking of her stiletto heels on the footpath. Hopefully she was racing towards answers. Moments later, she turned down a narrow arcade until she found herself outside Billy Veland's shoe repair shop.

She opened the door and walked inside. The shop was warm and stuffy. It smelt of leather and shoe polish. She pressed the bell on the counter and the man who came out from behind the black curtain was just as Jenny Choi had described. Jill flashed her ID at him. Billy Veland studied it for a moment then picked up a brown leather shoe and a polishing rag.

'What can I do for you?' he asked, not bothering to look up. 'I'm here about Robbie Calloway. Did you know him?'

Veland dipped the rag in the polish. 'He's the copper who jumped from the tower in Callan Park a couple of days ago, isn't he? I read about him in the newspapers.'

'Yes. But I mean did you know him personally?'

'I know a lot of people, Detective.'

'Don't be smart with me.' Jill put her hand on her hip. 'I'm not interested in the fact that you lend money to desperate people. I'm not even going to ask about the high interest rates you charge or the legality of what you do. All I want to know is,' she leaned across the counter to Veland, 'did Robbie Calloway owe you money? And if he did, how much?'

'Nothing.'

Jill scowled. 'What do you mean, nothing?'

Veland put the shoe down on the counter and looked up at Jill. 'Just as I said, Robbie didn't owe me a cent. He repaid his debt.'

Jill wrinkled her brow, surprised by the news. 'Okay, so how much *had* he owed you?'

'A ten with three zeros after it.'

Jill didn't react, but it was a lot of money on a cop's salary. 'You say he paid it back? When? How?'

'Cash, the day he killed himself, actually. Came in here with a big smirk on his face, carrying a backpack filled with one hundred dollar notes.'

'Where did he get the money?'

The boot maker shrugged. 'How the hell would I know? It's none of my business. But he did say he wouldn't need my services anymore. Said he was coming into some money.'

Just then, the door opened and a customer walked in carrying a pair of tan boots. Veland looked at the customer, smiled. 'Won't be a moment.' He looked back at Jill, raised his eyebrows. 'Now, is there anything else I can help you with?'

'Not right now, but I may be back with more questions.'

Veland gave her a slimy smile before turning his full attention to his customer.

Jill left the shop and adjusted her scarf. She'd hoped Robbie's death had something to do with Veland, that he'd give her answers. But now she had more questions. She wondered where all this was leading. How did Robbie come up with the money to repay Veland? She was beginning to question how well she knew Robbie.

Jill unlocked her car and slid into the driver's seat. After she inserted the key in the ignition, she turned up the heat and considered the idea that Robbie was expecting to come into some money. She wondered what that meant and then she remembered — his grandmother had died a couple months back. Perhaps the estate was about to be settled and the money had come through.

Jill released the hand brake and reversed out from the parking space. The wind was blowing a gale and thunderous clouds were moving in from the south. Jill drove out of the car park and made a fast turn into Longueville Road. She checked her side mirrors before she moved to the next lane. She sailed through the traffic lights and had just taken the exit ramp onto Pacific Highway when she slammed her foot on the brake. A truck had stalled two cars ahead of her. She'd been thinking about the inheritance money Robbie and Fin could expect from their grandmother's estate and hadn't been concentrating on the road ahead. She was too close to the car in front and she'd nearly rear-ended it. Brakes squealed and the car behind her sounded its horn, only just managing to stop.

'Shit.' Jill blew out a breath, knew she had to get her head in order...she'd nearly caused a pile-up.

'The boss's been looking for you,' Luke Rawlings said when Jill passed him on the stairs on her way to the detectives' room. 'And he's not in a good mood, something to do with that kid who was stabbed at the Interchange.'

Jill walked along the corridor and stood on the threshold of Rimis's office. She knocked on the open door. 'You wanted to see me?'

'Come in. Sit down. And close the door behind you.' Before Rimis could ask how she had got on with Scott Carver, she told him she'd gone to see Billy Veland.

'Veland? What the hell do you think you were do-ing talking to him?'

'I wanted to find out if Robbie owed him money.'

Rimis rubbed his neck. 'Alright then, what did you find out?'

'Veland told me Robbie repaid a ten thousand dol-lar loan the morning he died.'

'Sounds like Robbie was getting things in order be-fore he...' Rimis's voice trailed off.

Jill hadn't thought of that. Rimis was right. People did settle their affairs before suicide.

'Look Jill, you have to know when to quit. There were no witnesses, no evidence, nobody was with Robbie the night he died as far as we know, which means the only person who can tell us what really happened in that tower is Robbie. The coroner's office rang and his autopsy has been delayed. Even so, I don't expect there will be anything in it to suggest his death was caused by another person.' He leaned over his desk. 'I know it's hard, but you have to accept his death and move on.'

Maybe she was wrong.

Rimis continued. 'I want all your attention focused on the Red Cave Gang. There's a strong possibility Adam Lee or the Cheung family are linked to the gang. I want you to check with Rawlings on that hit and run…see if there's a possibility they're related. Not only will it make us look good for our quarterly figures but if the attack has anything to do with Vincent Wan, it's a chance to get him off the streets.'

# TWENTY-ONE

AFTER JILL HAD LEFT RIMIS'S office she spent the rest of the day catching up on the paperwork that had accumulated in her pigeonhole. She was burying herself in routine, trying not to think too much about Robbie or about Rimis and how pissed off she was with him. He was a fine one to give her a lecture on knowing when to quit. Had he forgotten the part he played in the Taggart case? Rimis was the only person who'd believed Kevin Taggart was a serial killer and it hadn't been for his perseverance, Taggart would be still walking the streets a free man.

Jill looked at the time on her phone and started the shutdown process on her computer. Five more minutes and her shift would be over.

She stood up and looked across the cubicle divider to Luke Rawlings's workstation in time to catch him logging off from his Facebook page.

'How's, Lucy Fletcher, the girl who was run down in Smith Street?' Jill asked.

'The doctors don't expect her to pull through.' Luke straightened his shoulders and ran his hands through his thick hair. A habit born from vanity. Luke was the snappiest dresser in the office. More Armani than Kelly Country. When Jill looked into his eyes she saw no compassion for the girl.

Luke had been in the graduating class ahead of her at the Academy and although they were both the same rank, it was clear he considered himself her senior.

'Looks as if it was more than a hit and run. The girl had rope burns on her wrists and ankles and bruising to her face and head. A set of skid marks was found on the road next to where she was found. Accident investigators from AIS are over there now carrying out a tyre mark analysis.'

Jill leaned on the partition and considered what Luke had said. 'So, she could have been running away from someone or something when she was hit by the car?'

'There's a good chance she was.' Luke leaned back on his chair and put his hands behind his head.

'Any witnesses?' Jill asked.

'An old couple on their way home from a night out. They live in Hercules Street, not far from where it happened.'

Jill reached over and pulled a map of the local government area for Chatswood off her partition and walked around to Luke's workstation. She picked up a green highlighter pen from his desk and pulled the cap off with her teeth.

'What are you doing?' Luke leaned forward and looked at the map.

'The old couple were on their way to their house in Hercules Street, you said?'

'Yeah.'

'And Lucy Fletcher. She was knocked over in Smith Street just around the corner from Douglas Avenue where David Cheung's body was found in the boot of his car.' Jill leaned over the map and ran the highlighter pen through the street names.

Rawlings looked at the scale. The streets are all within a six to eight kilometre radius of each other.

'What's with all the questions? It's not your case.'

Jill straightened up, looked at Rawlings. 'The boss wants me to work with you on it. It could be tied up with this Asian gang business.'

'He didn't say anything to me about it.'

'Don't be precious, Luke. I thought you'd be glad of the help.'

Rawlings grunted. Jill leaned over and looked back at the map. 'I wonder what the girl was doing in Smith Street? It's a pretty isolated part of Chatswood at that time of night. And what are the odds of her being run over at almost the same time as someone was stuffing David Cheung's body into the boot of his car?'

'It could be a coincidence.' Rawlings scratched his head, leaned over and looked at the map again.

'I don't believe in coincidences,' Jill said. She tapped the highlighter on her teeth. 'What did the old couple tell you? Did they get a plate?'

'They said the vehicle didn't have its headlights on and swerved a couple of times before it took off. It was too dark for them to see the license plate but they said they thought they saw something on the side of the road when they drove past, but they weren't sure. They thought it might have been a dog, but rang triple zero when they got home just in case.'

Jill replaced the lid on the highlighter.

'Now can I get back to eating my dinner?'

Jill looked down at the plastic container on Luke's desk. 'For God's sake, Luke what is that?'

'Kung Po Chicken.' Rawlings took a mouthful. 'It tastes better than it looks.'

Jill hoisted her backpack over her shoulder.

'Off to the gym?' he asked.

'Yeah, signed up at Crunch Fitness a week ago for that class you suggested. I probably won't be able to walk tomorrow; the instructor looks like he doesn't take prisoners.'

'Good luck.'

Jill smiled. 'I just might need it.'


Fifteen minutes later Jill walked into the gym class and immediately recognised the instructor she'd spoken to the previous week. He was broad-shouldered, powerful looking, with bleached blonde hair tied back in a short ponytail. Beneath the tattoos his arms were sinewy with muscle.

Jill had enrolled in the Warrior Class, a combination of heart-pumping cardio and intense strength training. With all that had happened during the past few days, the last thing she felt like was going to the gym but she'd paid for the class up front. Besides, the workout might help her burn off steam. She hoped the kick boxing class she'd been going to would hold her in good stead.

The room was filling up fast. Jill began with some stretches. She had one arm extended in the air when she saw him out of the corner of her eye. Rimis.

'I'm going to kill you, Luke bloody Rawlings,' she mumbled under her breath. He'd set her up. He must have known Rimis took this class. It occurred to her that she might still be able to slip away without being noticed, but it was too late. Nick Rimis was headed straight for her. A smile spread across his face as he approached her. He didn't miss a beat.

'Didn't know you were a member of the gym, Brennan.'

'I usually go to a kick boxing class closer to home.'

'Well, good to see you're taking your fitness seriously.'

Jill blushed, felt Rimis's eyes on her. She adjusted the waistline of her pink Lycra shorts, flicked her bra strap with a finger and moved to the back of the class. There was no way Nick Rimis was standing behind her, staring at her backside for the next forty-five minutes.

Fifteen minutes into the training, the instructor told them to grab a medicine ball and a partner. Before Jill had a chance to team up with someone Rimis was standing in front of her with a heavy, brown leather ball in his hands and a stupid grin on his face. He was enjoying this. She rearranged her pout to a smile. There was no sense blaming Rimis, it wasn't his idea, it had been Luke Rawlings's suggestion that she come to this gym and this particular class. Nick Rimis. He was more than her boss, he was a friend and despite his gruff exterior she had sensed on more than one occasion he had feelings for her that went beyond the welfare of a colleague.


When Jill arrived home to her empty apartment around eight o'clock she did her normal ritual of checking all the rooms before she took a shower. Luke Rawlings. He would have thought it was a great joke sending her off to the same gym class as Rimis. She didn't even know Rimis went to the gym. He'd been on a health kick a while back, but it hadn't lasted. Jill knew with the long hours, the erratic shifts and the effort it took to cook proper meals, it wasn't always easy to keep in shape. After the gym class, Rimis had asked if she wanted to go with him for something to eat but she'd said no and opted for take-away instead.

She put the container of Mongolian Lamb and fried rice she'd picked up on her way home into the microwave. While she waited for it to heat up, she poured herself a glass of Pinot Grigio. The dish was enough for two. It was like the take-away restaurants liked to rub in someone's single status. Everything was made for couples. Including the bottle of wine sitting on the kitchen counter.

She finished her glass of wine in three gulps, leaned her hip against the counter. Kevin Taggart. He was always in the background. The case had changed everything. The relationship with Nick Rimis had shifted from boss to friend. After Taggart had attacked her he'd sat by her bedside all night at the hospital. Then she thought of William Phillips. She wondered where he was now. The last she'd heard from him, he'd resigned from his job in a city law firm and had headed north with a surfboard attached to the roof racks of his Beemer. Did he ever think of her? She sighed. She'd thought they'd had something special until the night Taggart came to her apartment and ruined it all. When she was recovering in the hospital William had told her he couldn't handle knowing every day she went to work, she might not come home. Perhaps her no-dating-cops policy was flawed. Maybe, she should face facts. The majority of men she met were cops and they were certainly more likely to understand the job than any other guy.

She looked at the bottle of wine in front of her and poured herself another drink.

# TWENTY-TWO

Luke Rawlings adjusted his designer tie and knocked on Rimis's door. 'You got a minute, boss? I thought you'd want to hear the update on David Cheung.'

Rimis looked up from the file on his desk. 'Sit down, Rawlings. But before you tell me what you've got, I want Brennan working with you on the Lucy Fletcher case.'

'Yeah, Brennan told me.'

Rimis gave a nod. 'Brennan's been seconded to work on Asian gangs in the Chatswood area under Scott Carver's task force. Given Lucy Fletcher had restraint marks and taking into account her age, it's obvious her death was a result of more than a simple hit and run. This spate of attacks we've been having looks like it's escalating.' Rimis scratched his head and moved a pile of files to one side of his desk. 'I've asked area command for extra manpower.' Rimis looked at Rawlings. 'Tell me what you've got on David Cheung.'

'I went back to the Cheung's house and spoke to the neighbours. 'The kid, Benjamin, goes to St Pius X College. The school hasn't heard from him or his mother.'

'The family was obviously involved in something serious enough to cost David Cheung his life.' Rimis leaned into his desk. 'What about the neighbours in Douglas Avenue?'

'There's an old folks' home in the street and with the eighteenth birthday party and the footy game on television I think most people were inside with the curtains drawn. The music wasn't that loud, but loud enough for one neighbour to complain. The two uniforms that went to investigate didn't remember seeing the car on that occasion, but because the parents weren't home they decided to go back an hour later to check up on the kids. The party was over, and that's when they noticed the BMW.'

'Any forensics?' Rimis asked.

'The car's been impounded and the crime-scene techs are going over it now. There wasn't enough blood in the boot or the car to suggest he was killed in-situ. It looks like Cheung was killed elsewhere and the body dumped in the boot.'

'Well, follow up on it. Let me know as soon as you've got something. This hit and run, the attack on Adam Lee and Cheung's murder are all tied back to the Red Cave Gang, I'm sure of it. From this point on, all leave is cancelled. I want everyone's full attention on this.'

Jill was at her desk, staring at her computer screen. She was supposed to be looking at David Cheung's file, but instead she decided to try and track Robbie's car. She logged onto the Road and Maritime Authority website on a hunch. Robbie *had* sold his car. So, that was where he got the money to repay Billy Veland. Jill wasn't sure what to make of this latest piece of information. If anything, it fuelled the idea of a man tying up loose ends.

She was running out of motives and conspiracy theories.

# TWENTY-THREE

JILL ANSWERED HER PHONE. It was Katrina Andrel, the piranha.

'I was hoping we could meet for coffee. I'm in Chatswood and…'

'Look, if this is about Senior Constable Calloway, I'm really not interested in talking to you.'

Jill considered hanging up when the reporter cut in.

'Robbie was a friend of mine. He told me about you, the kind of person you are and I think it would be helpful if we could talk.'

'You knew Robbie?' Katrina Andrel had a reputation for being someone who went to great lengths for a story. Could she trust this woman? Was she playing her and if so, what was her angle? Was this a way to get her to talk?

Jill rubbed her eyes with the heels of her hands. Was it possible Katrina Andrel actually knew why Robbie might have taken his own life?

It was close enough to knock-off time to slip out without being noticed. Jill grabbed her coat and slung her bag over her shoulder. If Rimis ever found out she was talking to the reporter, he'd skin her alive.

The sky was a dirty dove-grey when Jill walked out on to Archer Street. She tightened her scarf around her neck and tucked her hands into her coat pockets. The temperature was dropping fast and it was getting dark. It was only days away from the winter solstice.

The café where she had arranged to meet Katrina Andrel was empty, apart from a group of schoolboys sitting at a table in the front section. Jill sidestepped their school backpacks and ordered a pot of lemongrass and ginger tea. She found a table facing the street, sat with her back to the wall and waited for Katrina Andrel to arrive. She sipped her tea, checked her phone.

When the chair opposite her scraped on the polished concrete floor Jill looked up. Katrina Andrel was standing in front of her dressed in a simple poppy-red coat over a pair of denim jeans.

Jill got to her feet and extended her hand. 'Detective Jill Brennan.'

'Katrina Andrel.'

The waitress arrived and Katrina ordered a pot of Darjeeling. The pause gave Jill a chance to assess the woman sitting across from her. Her face betrayed nothing. Men would find her attractive, even with the heavy make-up and the bleached blonde hair.

Jill took a sip of tea and put her cup down on the saucer. She got straight to the point. 'Can I ask how you got my name and how you knew I had been in a relationship with Robbie Calloway?'

Katrina gathered her coat around her and crossed her arms lightly against her chest. 'Let's just say a little bird.'

Jill rolled her eyes. A little bird called Constable Patullo, no doubt. He was practically panting at the sight of Andrel.

'I saw you at the scene. I asked around and I was given your name. I recognised it immediately. Robbie told me about you, about your relationship.' She paused. 'And it wasn't hard to find you; it was just a matter of making a phone call.' She leaned forward.

'Look Jill, before we go any further you should know how much Robbie thought of you.'

Jill knew how Robbie felt about her and she didn't need this woman to tell her. Jill kept her face impassive and waited for Andrel to fill the silence.

Andrel shrugged off her coat. 'I suppose I should start at the beginning. I didn't know Robbie that well, but even so, when I turned up last Friday night at Callan Park to cover the story it was a shock when I found out it was Robbie.'

Jill pulled out her notebook from her shoulder bag and Katrina shifted in her seat.

'You don't mind if I take notes do you? I've got a shocking memory.'

'I thought we might have this conversation off the record.' Katrina curled her lip to one side and went to grab her coat.

Jill put her notebook away and Katrina relaxed. 'How did you and Robbie meet?' Jill asked. 'Strangely enough, I met him at Callan Park.'

When Katrina's tea arrived she added two sachets of sugar to her cup and stirred. The movement was slow and methodical. She seemed uncertain, shy almost. This was a different Katrina to the one she saw last Friday night and Jill wondered what she was playing at.

Katrina looked up. 'A group of protesters staged a sit-in at the Wellness Centre at Callan Park back in February. They were meeting the Minister of Planning over the state government's decision to allow buildings earmarked for mental health services to be given over to other entities. I was sent there to report on the protest. There was a large police presence. It wasn't just the local area command, other commands had been called in to make sure things didn't get out of hand.'

Katrina placed the teaspoon on the saucer and sipped her tea. 'Robbie spoke to the camera crew and to me. Told us to tread lightly because tempers were running hot. We talked for a while, he flirted with me, I gave him my card and a few days later he phoned and invited me out. We had a lot in common. We weren't lovers or anything, we were just friends, but I had hoped we might…' Katrina riffled through her purse and pulled out a tissue, dabbing at her eyes with it. 'He told me his sister has mental health issues. Perhaps that would explain his attraction to Callan Park.'

Robbie had never told Jill about Fin's mental state, but maybe he wanted to keep it to himself. People were like icebergs. Nobody really knew what lay beneath the surface of another person's life, what parts of them they chose to keep hidden from public view. Before Jill had gone to see Fin, she had no idea she was mentally ill. Fin must have functioned well enough, because Robbie had mentioned she had some sort of a job in sales.

'Did you know Robbie had moved from his Collaroy apartment?' Jill asked.

'No, I didn't.' Andrel's eyes fixed on Jill. 'I wonder why he didn't tell me. Why he chose not to.'

Jill let Katrina Andrel sit with the news a bit and then said, 'So, tell me, when was the last time you saw him?'

'The Tuesday before he died. We met for drinks. He was agitated and when I asked him about it he said things were happening in his life, personal things, and that they were intruding on his work. He'd asked his boss for time off, but he wouldn't give it to him — they were short staffed and had a blow-out of their case load.'

Jill frowned. 'What sort of things? Did he say?'

'That's just it, Jill. He never told me. I can call you Jill, can't I? Or should I call you Detective?'

Jill resisted pointing out that Andrel had already called her Jill a couple of times. She forced a smile. 'No, Jill's fine. Did he ever mention any cases he was working on?'

'Sometimes, but not until they were reported in the news. He was very careful about what he said to me and I was careful not to compromise his position as a police officer.'

Sounded like Robbie.

Katrina leaned forward. 'There's something not quite right, don't you think? You can sense it too, I can tell. You wouldn't be asking me quite so many questions if you thought Robbie had simply killed himself.'

Jill wasn't about to confide in a journalist who she'd just met and besides, she knew Katrina Andrel's reputation for hunting down a story. 'What were your impressions of Robbie during the time you knew him? You must be very good at summing people up. Journalists have a way of getting people to talk.' Perhaps Katrina could shed some light on Robbie's more recent past, a chunk of his life that was elusive to Jill.

'I wouldn't say he was unhappy. Robbie lived for his work and on the surface he was always cheerful, always the joker. And as you'd know, he never had a bad word to say about anybody.' She stared into her cup, looked up. 'Deep down, I think Robbie was a man who was carrying a burden. I thought it might have been his sister. He told me she was drinking heavily. He tried to get her to go to AA or see a counsellor, but she refused.' Katrina toyed with the handle of her cup. 'But I could be wrong; it could have been something else entirely. But whatever was troubling him, he didn't want to share it with anybody.'

Silence.

'A secret you mean?'

'Yes, a secret.'

# TWENTY-FOUR

JILL POURED MORE TEA INTO her cup and wondered if Robbie had gotten in over his head with his gambling debts. It was true, he'd paid off Billy Veland, but he could have owed money to somebody else.

'What do you think he was doing at Callan Park?' Jill asked.

Katrina stirred her tea and stared past Jill as if thinking what to say next. 'No idea, I've been wondering the same thing.' She looked up. 'Robbie told me his father had epilepsy or was it schizophrenia? Maybe Robbie had a fit or something. Was there anything in the autopsy report about it?'

'We're still waiting on the autopsy. Robbie's case is low priority.'

Katrina nodded, dabbed at her eyes with her fingers. 'I'm sorry, but I can't believe Robbie would have taken his own life.' Katrina leaned in as if sharing a confidence, she lowered her voice. 'Have you considered he may have been pushed?'

Jill was surprised, maybe even a little relieved, that someone else was following the more sinister line of thought. But she couldn't let her guard down, not with a journo. 'There's nothing much I can tell you, without an autopsy report.' Katrina Andrel could just be digging, hoping to find a story. It took a moment for Jill to compose herself. She shrugged. 'There's no evidence to suggest it was anything other than suicide.' Jill changed the subject. 'Is there anything else you can tell me?'

'I know Robbie was worried about Fin, worried what she might do.' Katrina Andrel paused and sipped her tea thoughtfully. 'I think he was at the end of his tether with her.'

'What do you mean?'

'Fin was depressed; drinking too much, hanging out with the wrong crowd. Robbie found out she'd lost her job. He told me he was worried there might have been something more serious going on and he'd been trying to get her help. But she'd refused.'

'What exactly did he think was wrong with her?'

'He didn't say, but he told me he'd visited a few mental health sites and had been reading text books on behavioural problems.'

'What about drugs? Do you think Fin or Robbie was using? He never touched them when I was with him but…'

'Robbie? No, definitely not, he was scared of them. He told me he'd been tempted once…after an addict told him taking heroin was like sitting on your mother's lap. It made you feel loved and like no one would ever hurt you.'

Jill raised her eyebrows.

'I'm not sure about Fin, though. Robbie let something slip once and I got the impression she was involved in something illegal.'

'What did Robbie say?' Jill asked.

'I think it was to do with someone she was seeing.'

Jill was surprised Katrina knew so much about the Calloways, considering she'd only known them both for a short time. A pang of jealousy hit her; it appeared Katrina Andrel knew more about Robbie's life than she did.

Katrina continued. 'Robbie was outraged mentally ill people were living on the streets because of a lack of state government funding. He said Callan Park should never have closed and he couldn't understand why the Master Plan hadn't been approved.' Katrina's phone rang and she looked at the caller ID. 'Look, I have to take this.' She stood to leave.

'One last question,' Jill said.

Katrina answered the call. 'Give me a second, will you Naomi.' She pressed hold on her phone and looked back to Jill. 'Yes, what did you want to ask me?' She picked up her coat and bag and placed a five-dollar note and some loose change on the table.

Jill had decided since first meeting Katrina Andrel at Callan Park that she didn't like the woman. Yet she had brought up the idea Robbie may have been pushed. Why? Was she an ally or was she involved in some way? She felt like saying: yes, I have considered Robbie was pushed and who's to say you weren't the one up there with him? But instead she decided to find out if she had an alibi.

'Where were you the night Robbie died, before you turned up in the news van?'

'I was meeting one of my sources.'

'Can you give me a name?'

'Sorry, Jill, I never reveal my sources, not even to my editor.'

'Can anyone else confirm your whereabouts?'

'I have no alibi, if that's what you're asking.' She narrowed her eyes. 'So, you agree with me? You don't think Robbie's death was suicide.' She gave Jill a satisfied smile.

Jill kept her cool, attempted a smile. 'No, it's just one of those questions I have to ask. Thank you by the way. I appreciate you contacting me.'

Katrina tugged her ear. 'I just wanted to help in any way I could. Robbie was special.'

Jill nodded and Katrina went back to her phone. 'Sorry, Naomi...' She walked out of the café, giving Jill a quick wave.

The waitress was wiping down the next table and Jill asked her for a strong black coffee — her first for a while. She'd thought giving up caffeine would help her insomnia, but so far her abstinence had had no effect. She was also tempted to ask for a vanilla slice or one of the Portuguese tarts she liked so much, especially given she'd skipped lunch, but she resisted. While she waited for her coffee to arrive, she went over the conversation she'd just had with Katrina Andrel. There was something not quite right. What was it about the woman that unsettled her? Was it the way she swept out of the café, the fake tears at the start of their conversation? She wondered if Katrina Andrel was playing with her and decided to run a background check. She wanted to confirm her story that she'd covered the protest at Callan Park.

# TWENTY-FIVE

AFTER JILL LEFT THE CAFÉ she drove to Manly Police Station. DI Perris had stonewalled her on the phone, but maybe a personal visit and a quiet chat with Robbie's partner would be more fruitful. Unfortunately, she'd been dead wrong. The whole team was out on jobs and no one else was talking. It had been a long shot. A long shot that hadn't paid off, and if her visit got back to Rimis…

Jill returned to Chatswood station in time to see two uniforms wrestling with a handcuffed youth in jeans and a grey hoodie. Jill stood back, opened the door for them, and made a quick side step to avoid being kicked.

'Sorry,' said one of the constables.

Jill walked up the stairs behind them and when she got to the detectives' room she swiped her security card, walked in and threw her shoulder bag on her desk. She sat down in her chair, picked up a pen and rolled it between her thumb and forefinger. The drive back from Manly had taken longer than she'd expected. With the opening of the Spit Bridge it had added fifteen minutes to the trip.

Rawlings had been on the phone when she'd walked in. When he ended his call he leaned his elbow on the workstation divider. 'The boss has been looking for you. Wants you in his office ASAP.'

Jill sighed and threw her pen on the desk.

'What's up, Brennan?' Luke said. 'You look beat.'

Jill didn't realise her lack of sleep showed. 'Got a few things on my mind, Luke.' She looked at her phone messages.

'It's not Robbie Calloway, is it?'

She shot him a look. 'Mind your business.'

'If it is Calloway, a word of advice.'

'I don't need your advice, Luke.' Jill was still mad at him because of the business with Rimis and the gym.

'Well, like it or not I'm going to give it to you anyway. My gut says this is political. Land grabs, developers, and shady politicians, that sort of thing. Everyone knows how valuable Callan Park is as a redevelopment site. Sixty-six acres of prime riverfront land. Mighty valuable real estate no matter what you think of land developers. And the state government still hasn't approved the Master Plan for the site. Could explain why that reporter Katrina Andrel is sniffing around and why the boss and the DCI have warned you off. If you keep poking your nose in where it shouldn't be, you might find something you weren't expecting. Might even affect your career.'

Jill wondered if there was any merit in what Rawlings was saying. If you ignored his ego, she had to admit he was a good officer. 'Thanks for the advice as always, Luke.' Jill winked. 'I'll keep it in mind.'

'Well, don't say I didn't warn you.'

She didn't have much time for Rawlings, but she had heard what he was trying to tell her. And she remembered the words of warning she'd received from Rimis and Scott Carver well enough to know she probably risked a formal reprimand by going against direct orders from a detective inspector and an area commander.

Jill walked out of the room and headed down the corridor to Rimis's office. Was it her imagination or was everyone looking at her? Choi lowered her eyes when she passed her in the corridor outside Rimis's office.

Jill found herself standing outside Rimis's door. It was closed. She heard muted voices. She knocked.

Rimis called her in. 'Come in Detective and close the door.' He'd called her Detective. This was serious. Jill sat down.

'Scott Carver phoned me. We're both concerned about the obsession you seemed to have developed over the death of Robbie Calloway.'

Obsessed with Robbie? Of course she was obsessed.

She met Rimis's gaze. Someone killed Robbie, pushed him from that tower and I'm going to find out who that person is, no matter what the consequences.

'You're supposed to be working the Asian gangs, but instead Choi is run ragged doing your work and hers. And where the hell have you been?'

She gulped. 'I went to Manly. I wanted to see if I could talk to some of the detectives who knew Robbie. I thought they might be able to tell me if...'

'Shit, Brennan. Is this how you behave after Carver handpicked you and Choi to work on the task force into Asian gangs? And I know you went to Manly because DI Perris spotted you. Instead of coming to me, he phoned the Commissioner's office. Everyone, including you, knows the Commissioner's directive for silence on Calloway's suicide. He's being pressured by the Premier to keep a low profile on PTSD.'

Jill sat down and crossed her arms. Her world was about to change because of a single phone call.

There was a tense silence for a moment. Rimis took another tack. 'Your failure to accept the evidence that suggests Calloway committed suicide is something that surprises me. You're acting irrationally, you seemed to have lost all sense of reason.' Rimis ran his hand over the back of his neck. 'Both Carver and I have warned you, keep going the way you are and you could find yourself back in uniform.'

Jill froze.

Rimis looked at her. 'You've got twenty-six days' annual leave owing and I want you take a week's leave. Go away somewhere, rest, sleep, go for walks. Read a book or ten.' He paused, still holding her gaze. 'And before you come back, I want you to undertake a full mental assessment to make sure you're fit to perform your duties.'

What did Rimis just say? A mental assessment? He thinks I'm crazy?

Jill expected a reprimand, but not this. So this is how her career trajectory was to end? All the hard work, the sacrifices for it to end back in uniform or stuck behind a desk somewhere in a corner next to a steel, three-door filing cabinet. Jill felt the hot sting behind her eyes. Her obsession with Robbie's death may cost not only her reputation but she could risk the only thing that mattered to her: her job as a detective.

# TWENTY-SIX

MOST NIGHTS OTTO'S BAR WAS full of staff from the morgue and cops who worked close-by or were on their way home, but tonight is was quiet. Rimis had had a stressful day, no thanks to Jill Brennan. He was still fuming over her refusal to listen to reason over Robbie Calloway's suicide. And the news about Fiona and this baby business had put him in a bad mood all week. He ordered another glass of wine, put all thoughts of Jill Brennan aside and thought about his ex-wife instead. When Fiona had left him it had come out of the blue. Why were husbands always the last to know? He had no idea she'd been so miserable. Women. He should be happy for her; after all, now she had the life she'd always dreamt of. Nice home, doting husband and the baby she and Rimis had talked about but never got around to having.

What sort of father would he have made, anyway? Lousy. Shift work, callouts during the night. No, he'd made his decision. Just him from now on, him and the job. It was enough. He finished his third glass of wine and returned to the newspaper article he'd been reading before thoughts of Fiona and the baby had sidetracked him. A Queensland man had reported his wife missing and when questioned by the police about the scratches on his face, he'd told them he'd cut himself shaving with a blunt razor blade, not once, but three times.

Rimis shook his head. 'Must think we're a bunch of idiots.'

'It's never a good idea to drink alone, even worse when you're caught talking out loud to yourself.'

Rimis swivelled around on the barstool. It was Greer Ross. He stood up and grabbed his coat from the stool next to him. He noticed her clothing. She was dressed in a knee-length skirt and a jumper that emphasised her full figure. 'You look nice,' he said, regretting the remark almost immediately. Greer Ross had the habit of giving him a frosty reception whenever they met during the course of their work. She may have considered it a sexist comment. He looked at the stubborn set of her chin and was relieved when she smiled.

Greer sat down on the stool next to him. She leaned into the bar and crossed her legs.

The perfume she was wearing reminded Rimis of honey and berries. 'I haven't seen you in here before,' Rimis said.

'I've had a particularly bad day. Actually, make that days. I felt like a drink before I went home to an empty apartment.'

Rimis raised his eyebrows. Greer Ross was an attractive, intelligent woman and even without a wedding ring on her finger he was surprised there wasn't someone waiting for her at home. While he had just entered his forties he guessed she was well into her thirties.

'I know that feeling.' Rimis caught the bartender's eye. 'What would you like to drink?'

'A glass of Shiraz would be nice.'

'I think we deserve a bottle, don't you?' Rimis had already decided to take a taxi home, pick the car up in the morning. He ordered a bottle of 2011 Hunter Valley Shiraz and when he turned back to her, he noticed her studying him. 'What?'

'What did you mean by you know that feeling? A bad day or going home to an empty apartment?'

'Both, I suppose,' Rimis said.

A few moments later, the bartender set down the bottle and two wine glasses in front of Rimis. Rimis looked at the label and poured. He swirled the wine and raised his glass. 'Cheers.' He wasn't sure what he was toasting to.

'Cheers.'

Rimis realised this was the first time they'd spoken to each other in a social situation. Each time they met, a silent partner was present. A permanently silent partner.

Rimis found himself staring at Greer over the top of his glass. Her glossy dark hair was pulled back with a clip. It cascaded down her shoulders and back. 'Don't know how you do the job you do,' he said.

'We're even. I don't know how you do your job.' She raised her glass to him and took another mouthful of wine.

Rimis's stomach was complaining, growling for food. He leant over and grabbed a bowl filled with mixed nuts. If he had any sense he'd head home, now. He was about to make his excuses to Greer when she asked him what his zodiac sign was.

He cocked his head to one side and looked at her. 'Taurus, why?'

'My mother's an astrologist. She also reads palms.'

Rimis laughed. 'You're kidding me?'

'No, I'm not kidding and why are you laughing? My mother takes her work very seriously and a lot of her predictions about people are spot on.'

'Next, you'll be telling me you've got a voodoo doll in your handbag and you're about to stick pins into me.'

'You're making fun of me now.'

'No, I'm not.'

Greer raised her eyebrows.

'You're an extremely interesting person, Greer Ross. I find you very attractive.' Rimis felt the lump in his throat. He should never drink on any empty stomach. Makes you say stupid things. He got to his feet, took a few more sips from his glass and placed it on the bar. 'Sorry.' He cleared his throat, feeling embarrassed by his sudden outpouring of emotion. 'See you later.' He turned to leave but she grabbed his arm.

'I'm a Scorpio,' she said.

Rimis met her eyes, hesitated, but then sat back down again. 'Tell me about Scorpios,' he said with renewed interest.

She let go of his arm and rested her hand on the stem of her glass. 'You really want to know?'

'Of course.' Rimis was more than a little interested in what Greer had to say about herself, the detective's curiosity was rising to the surface, the part of his personality that needed to solve riddles and uncover secrets.

'Passion, desire, power. I'd say that sums Scorpios up pretty well.'

Rimis wondered if there was something in this astrology business, after all. He moved his stool a little closer to Greer.

'The biggest challenge in life for Scorpios is choosing between the power of love and the love of power. They wear a mask and say 'no' when they really mean, 'yes.' When they find true love they can be the most faithful of all partners, but fall out with a Scorpio; watch out, they never forgive or forget.'

'Never forgive or forget, hey? Scary.'

Greer slipped her hand onto his thigh.

Rimis made no attempt to move it. 'I'm surprised you're sitting here talking to me. I had a feeling you didn't like me very much.'

'I take my job seriously, Inspector, I can't afford distractions. When I'm at work, I work.'

Rimis swirled his wine, dived in. 'Am I a distraction, Doctor Ross?'

'As a matter of fact, yes, you are.'

Rimis emptied his glass and put it aside.

'A top up?'

Rimis nodded and leaned into the bar. 'So then, tell me something about yourself apart from being a Scorpio. I already know you're a South African doctor who takes her work seriously.'

Greer filled his glass. Her long hair swung forward and she brushed it back with her fingertips. 'I'm the eldest of two girls, born and raised in Cape Town. Mother English, father, South African doctor of Indian extract. I studied at the University of The Western Cape and ended up working as a forensic pathologist with the Western Cape Forensic Pathology Service.' Greer took a mouthful of wine. 'I met an Australian mining engineer, married him, which I might add was the biggest mistake of my life. We moved to Australia and lived in Western Australia until our divorce. We went our separate ways after five years of marriage. And now, voilà here I am, living in a big city, with lots of work and no friends.'

Rimis noticed how sad Greer looked — not that he could talk. After Fiona walked out on him, his life had become an emotional dust bowl. And now, with this baby business, he was faced with the prospect that he'd never have the package of wife, mortgage and kids. He had a hard time even remembering what it felt like to wake up in the morning with a woman by his side.

He looked at Greer and wondered if it was the drink, but he'd never seen her look so fragile or so beautiful. Why did he find vulnerable women so attractive? He had a sudden urge to hold her in his arms and stroke her hair.

'What about you, Nick, are you married?'

'I was. Fiona. She was a police officer, surprise, surprise. She left the force, thought I should too. Then one day she gave me an ultimatum — the job or the marriage.' Rimis looked at his watch. He couldn't believe the time. It was almost 10 pm. He hadn't meant to drink so much. 'It's getting late, I should go,' he said. 'I've got a busy day tomorrow.' He wondered if it sounded like an excuse to her. He'd been out of the dating game for so long he didn't know the rules anymore.

'I should be going as well,' Greer said. 'I haven't got my car; it's in for a service. We can share a taxi, if you like.'

'What a great idea.'

# TWENTY-SEVEN

THE DOORS TO THE LIFT opened. Greer Ross led Rimis down the carpeted hall to her apartment. He stood behind her, wrapped one arm around her waist and rested his head on her shoulder while she looked for the keys in her handbag. When the door opened, they fell into the apartment. Rimis kicked the door shut and took her in his arms. Greer collapsed against the nearest wall and felt the give of her breasts against his chest. She moaned and he kissed her hard, their tongues wet and sour from the wine.

Greer unzipped her skirt and let it fall off her hips, then pulled her jumper over her head. Taking Rimis's hand, she led him towards her bedroom. She turned on a reading light. Rimis stood by the foot of the bed watching her, with a look on his face that said he wasn't sure he should even be here.

Greer wondered how many drinks Rimis had had before she'd shown up at Otto's but from the glow of his cheeks she knew she'd drunk considerably less than him. She wondered if the night would end in disaster. Was he even capable?

She removed her red, lacy underwear, walked up to him and slowly, carefully she undid the buttons on his shirt, removed it, noticed a scar from a bullet wound on his right shoulder. When she touched it, he flinched. She wondered about it for a moment but decided to wait. She would ask him how he got it later.

She ran her hands over his muscled chest, kissed the matted black chest hair showing the first signs of grey. She managed to remove his shoes and socks before he fell onto the bed. With his knees spread apart, the sight of the bulge in his trousers made her catch her breath. 'Eish!' she said in Afrikaans. She slid her hand down the front of his trousers while she fumbled with his belt buckle with the other.

'Hang on,' he said and reached into his trouser pocket. Greer was surprised when he pulled out four foil-wrapped packets. 'The vending machine at Otto's,' he whispered in her ear. 'Got a few extra, just in case.'

'Let me.' She smiled, ripped one of the packets open with her teeth, straddled him, shivered, gazed down at him, at his mouth soft and open, eyes suddenly focused. She felt the stirring of his hunger.

He grabbed her, rolled her onto her back, she bit his lip and he caressed her full breasts. The misery and tension of her job blurred into the background as he worked cleverly and tenderly on her. His warm, naked body was eager to please, his kisses muffled her cries, she felt herself clench. 'Ek wil dit hard,' she groaned. 'Baie hard.'


Rimis woke with a start. His head felt thick and heavy, his mouth tasted like he'd been sucking on sweaty socks all night. He slipped from the bed and after he'd been to the bathroom, he went and stood by the window. It was just before dawn. The curtains were pulled back and it was raining heavily outside, another bitter winter's morning. There was an occasional mirror-like flash in the distance followed by a low rumbling of thunder. He rubbed the sleep from his eyes and gazed down at the street below. The streetlights cast glimmering shadows onto the wet bitumen, the gutters overflowed with water, the storm water drains were blocked.

An occasional taxi whooshed along the street, headlights blazing through the misty rain. How good it felt to be standing naked in Greer Ross's bedroom, listening to the beat of his own heart and remembering the warmth of the bed he'd just left. He looked around the room. He had other things on his mind last night and hadn't taken much notice of Greer's bedroom. He admired her taste; the room had African elements to it. The walls were painted a vibrant red-orange and the bedspread matched the wall colour. Two zebra-print pillows had fallen onto the floor during the night.

He studied the sensuous curve of Greer's spine, her smooth dusky skin, her thick hair spread across the pillow. There was something deeply sensuous about the contrast of the colour of the walls and the bedspread against the silky sheen of her naked body. It was wild and exotic and the sight of her aroused him. He was tempted to return to her bed but thought twice about it. He knew it was going to be awkward either way. Awkward if he stayed, awkward if he left without waking her. She looked so peaceful lying there, the last thing he wanted to do was wake her. He grabbed his clothes from the floor, pulled on his trousers and buttoned up his shirt. He looked at her one last time, and then quietly left her apartment.

# TWENTY-EIGHT

JILL LAY STILL, LISTENING to the silence, watching the shadow of the trees outside her bedroom window. She had been awake for hours.

She rolled over and looked at the time on her iPhone. Six-fifteen. Normally she would've been at work by now, but she was on annual leave... yeah, right. She buried her head in the covers. It had been another agonising night of fitful sleep, guilt and loss. At least she hadn't woken this morning from one of her nightmares. She rolled out of bed and went to the bathroom.

She stood in front of the mirror and examined her body. Six days since Robbie's death and the weight had fallen off her like melting snow. Yesterday she'd renewed her membership at the local gym, had taken up running again, something she'd let go when she'd started working double shifts. She was hoping to build muscle and improve her physical strength, and who knew, the exercise might help lift her mood.

Jill loved her job but there were times when she dreamed about escaping the life she'd built for herself. What was it her father used to say to her? You could run away from bad situations but not from who you were.

Perhaps he was right to have objected to her joining the force. Had he seen something lacking in her? A trait perhaps, a trait needed to cope with the violence and death she witnessed as a police detective? She sighed. If only Mickey was still alive. If only she had a mother who she could seek comfort from, talk to about how she was feeling. Too many 'ifs and onlys.'

With a week's leave ahead of her she'd already decided she wasn't going to be idle and sit around the apartment moping. Last night she'd gone onto the Sydney Morning Herald's web site and checked their archives and found the story Katrina Andrel had written on the protest at Callan Park.

This morning she would get back to her habit of beginning each day with a run to the beach, and then home for a shower. And after breakfast, she'd sit in front of her laptop and do some background searches on Robbie's family. Then, if she was in the mood, she'd listen to her Spanish CDs and practice getting her accent right. So much had happened this past week — Asian gangs, Robbie's death, the increase in the station's case loads, Lucy Fletcher, David Cheung's murder and the sudden disappearance of his family.

She wasn't looking forward to speaking to the police counsellor. After she'd recovered physically from her ordeal with Kevin Taggart she'd been sent to see her. And now, less than six months later, she would be seeing her again.

She closed her eyes for a minute and asked herself how she would perform this time around when her feelings were under scrutiny? She found herself questioning her judgement. What if Robbie really did commit suicide? It would have all been for nothing.

Jill poured herself a glass of water and returned to her bedroom to get dressed. It had been raining earlier but for now there was a break in the weather. She grabbed her track pants from the corner of the room and found her fleece, running shoes and socks under her bed. She tied her hair up in a high ponytail, grabbed her keys, deadlocked the front door on her way out and ran down the two flights of stairs. She did some stretches before she turned down the road towards Bondi Beach, warming up first with a jog. The streets were wet and deserted; it was still dark and the sun wasn't due to show itself for at least another fifteen minutes.

Jill had been running steadily for twenty minutes before she pushed herself harder, alternating jogging with short sprints. With the sun creeping over the horizon she ran along the promenade and onto the wide concrete steps to the beach. Her running shoes sank into the powdery sand and slowed her pace. Her thighs ached. When she reached the water's edge, she stopped, caught her breath and looked out at the rolling surf, remembering how she and her father had often come down here to surf. She sighed. It was the beginning of another day. There must have been winter days by the beach with her father but she couldn't remember them, she only remembered the sun, the sand and the surf. She walked along the tide line, stopping occasionally to pick up a shell or a pebble. There was no wind and the water slid onto the beach, the waves barely breaking. If only her life was that serene.

# TWENTY-NINE

IT WAS 6 AM WHEN Rimis stepped out of the shower and grabbed a towel. He was distracted by thoughts of Greer lying naked in his arms, her glistening skin, her round, firm breasts cupped in his hands. He remembered how good she'd felt against him. What was it about her that excited him so much? Those dewy brown eyes of hers, her firm breasts or the idea that, like him, she was alone and hadn't had sex for some time?

He dried himself off and struggled to push all thoughts of her out of his mind. He put on a fresh shirt and tie and after he brushed his teeth he studied himself in the mirror. He was a stubborn, gruff cop, efficient at his job yet still young enough to be interesting. Truth was, he was a divorced man who wore his loneliness on his face like an empty glass on a bar. He should stop hanging around Otto's, get out more, and take up golf. He laughed at himself: Golf?

When he caught a glimpse of the time on the kitchen clock, he realised he needed to get a move on. He finished his coffee, surprised by how good he felt, despite a slight hangover and a sense of disappointment in himself. Nick Rimis lived his life by a set of rules. It was the only way he could do the job. But last night he broke his number one rule — never sleep with a colleague, a friend or the partner of a friend.

By the time he arrived at the station Rimis's head was pounding. He took a couple of paracetamol, considered taking a third. He sat back in his chair with his hands behind his head and thought of Greer. What had he been thinking sneaking out on her like that this morning? Or maybe that was his problem. He hadn't been thinking at all. Shit, Rimis you're such an idiot. He ran his hand through his hair and looked down at the pile of paperwork in front of him.

Rimis had always worked long hours, taken the job seriously but when Fiona left he'd worked even harder, as if the extra shifts would in some way compensate for his loneliness. The upside had been his promotion from detective sergeant to detective inspector, the downside was that he'd worked himself senseless, concentrated so much on other people's problems, there was little time left to brood on his own. He'd thought that if he was busy and dog-tired he wouldn't mind the self-imposed celibacy. But after last night, he realised he'd been mistaken. The dam walls had broken and the desire he'd turned his back on had returned with a vengeance.

He took a deep breath and looked down at the pile of phone messages in front of him. After he pushed them to one side, he refreshed his computer screen and looked at his emails, deleted half of them unread, and immediately felt better.

One email he'd noticed and not deleted was from Scott Carver. Rimis liked the area commander. He was a man's man and a good officer. He'd been fast-tracked like Brennan, had a double degree in psychology and law and had come from a family of long-serving police officers. But Scott Carver had one downfall. He was a stickler for rules and regulations — everything was by the book with Carver.

Rimis pulled a pack of mints from his drawer and put his feet on his desk. To take his mind off his thumping headache, he thought again about how good it had been last night with Greer, but also how complicated his life had now become. There could never be a repeat performance. He looked down at his mobile phone on his desk. Twice he'd gone to ring her but had changed his mind. If it had been any woman other than Greer Ross who he'd had mind-blowing sex with, he would have called her by now and made a time to see her again, but Greer Ross wasn't any woman. She was a colleague. Last night had been a lapse in judgement — business and pleasure didn't mix. Fiona was a testament to that.

What had she said about Scorpios? They never forgive or forget. It was going to be hard working with her without thinking of honey and berries and the touch of her skin under his hands. He was going crazy with the thought of her.

A knock at the door saved him from himself, his feet fell from the desk and he sat upright in his chair. It was Jenny Choi. She was wearing another one of her ridiculous outfits. Today it was a hot pink skirt paired with a black spotted top and black stockings. He wondered if he should have a word to her about toning down her outfits, but thought better of it.

'You don't look well, boss.'

'Never mind that, Choi,' he snapped. 'What do you want?'

'It's about Benjamin Cheung and his alleged attack on Adam Lee.'

'Well out with it.'

'I find it hard to believe Benjamin Cheung attacked Adam Lee, especially with a knife. I've been doing some digging. Benjamin's not the type of boy to be running around in gangs or pulling knives on people.'

'Maybe he's the brains and there are other kids involved,' Rimis said.

'His teachers at St Pius didn't paint him as the brainy type. Not the sharpest tool in the shed, I think was the term they used.' Choi continued. 'The family lives in Northbridge. We searched the boy's bedroom with a relative's permission, but didn't find anything. And they were adamant Benjamin had nothing to do with Adam Lee's stabbing. I also asked around the Chinese community. Nobody's heard from either Benjamin or his mother since the night David Cheung was murdered…or if they have, they're not talking.'

'What about this girl involved in the hit and run? Lucy Fletcher,' Rimis asked. 'Jill was supposed to be looking into a possible link. Don't suppose she mentioned it to you or Rawlings before taking leave.' Rimis tried to hide his annoyance.

'Rawlings said she was looking at the location.' Choi cleared her throat. 'But I don't think she got very far with it.'

No, because she was too busy chasing dead leads on Robbie Calloway. Again, Rimis checked his anger. 'How's the girl doing?'

'No change. She's still in an induced coma. Her parents reported her missing a week ago. Seems there was trouble at home. She didn't get along with the dad.'

Rimis gave a nod. 'Jill might be onto something with the locations. Smith Street is only a few blocks from where David Cheung and his car were found,' Rimis said. 'I'll get Rawlings to look into it. I want you to go and speak to Lucy Fletcher's parents again. See if you can find out more about what she was doing in that part of Smith Street late at night and if they think anyone might have been after her for any reason…and if there's any explanation for those restraint marks. She might have been into something unsavoury. And speak to uniform, see if they've got anything further to add.'

'Will do.' Jenny stood to leave but turned around before she reached the door. 'Jill did a good job with Adam Lee, got him to talk. He wouldn't even look at me.'

Must have been the pink skirt and black stockings, probably scared the kid half to death.

'Yeah, Brennan's like a dog with a bone when she latches onto something. Lee didn't stand a chance.'

# THIRTY

JILL TOOK A BITE FROM her Vegemite toast and washed it down with strong tea. The run to the beach and back had cleared her head and the self-pity she'd been feeling earlier had been replaced by anger. Nick Rimis might think she was crazy and unreliable, but she'd worked too hard for it to fall apart now. With this enforced leave, she'd dig deep and come up with the evidence to prove Robbie hadn't taken his life.

Once dressed, Jill sat down on the lounge with her laptop and glanced across at *The Morning Show* on the television. She picked up the remote and turned the volume to low, and then double-clicked on the folder she'd created on Robbie.

With no other real leads, she decided to start from scratch — their childhood. Robbie and Fin had gone to live with their grandmother after their parents had died in a car accident. She needed to speak to someone who knew Robbie and Fin when they were children and knew their grandmother. It could be just a coincidence, but around the time the grandmother died Robbie's behaviour changed; at least according to Fin. It was a long shot but something in Robbie and Fin's past may explain what led Robbie to his death and explain Fin's strange behaviour.

Jill tried to remember if Robbie had ever mentioned where his grandmother had lived. She thought it was Katoomba. Calloway was not a common name so when she checked the white pages she found two

Calloways in Sydney; one in Pendle Hill and the other in Balgowlah. There was only one listing in Katoomba. She wrote down the address and phone number. She dialled the number but it was disconnected. It was worth trying the neighbour, they may know something. She did another address look-up, got the name, and then used it to find the number. When she made the call, there was no answer. She tried the same procedure again, but this time a few doors down from where Grace Calloway had lived. Someone answered on the first ring.

'Hello?' The voice was low, male.

'Yes, hello. My name's Detective Jill Brennan. I'm calling from Chatswood Police. I'm looking for someone who might have known a Mrs Grace Calloway.'

'Yeah, I knew Gracie. The wife and I went to her funeral.'

'Can I have your name please, sir?'

'Yeah, it's Allan, Allan Briggs.'

'Mr Briggs, can I ask how long you've lived in Milton Street?'

'About five years, came up to the Mountains to retire after I left the job at the steelworks down south.'

So Allan Briggs would never have met Robbie and Fin. They would have already left Katoomba by then. 'Is there anyone still living in the street who might have known the Calloways from before 2001?'

'Let me think. There's Maureen Hardcastle. She was Gracie's next-door neighbour. I remember speaking to her at the funeral. But she's not living there anymore. The family shuffled her off to a nursing home, she was having trouble with her memory.'

'I don't suppose you know which nursing home?'

'Haven't a clue, sorry love.'

Jill thanked him for his help and a few phone calls later she found Maureen Hardcastle at the Burlington Aged Care Home in Katoomba.

Jill thought about the police shows she watched on television. There were similarities to real policing, but it was never that straightforward, a murder investigation could take months or years to solve. In some cases, the crime went unsolved. The script writers of the shows made it look so easy — a person is murdered, a witness comes forward, a chase ensues, a twist, maybe a red herring or two thrown in for good measure, and an hour later the bad guy is behind bars. An hour…yeah, that'd be nice.

To regain her credibility Jill had to find proof Robbie had been pushed, or at least proof he'd fallen accidentally, from the clock tower. Maureen Hardcastle might be just the person to help. Jill drove across the Parramatta River and followed the GPS prompts to the entrance of the motorway. When she drove onto the M4 she put her foot down. She'd rung through to the nursing home before she'd left the outskirts of Sydney. Maureen Hardcastle would be expecting her, if she remembered.

# THIRTY-ONE

THE COMMON ROOM OF THE nursing home smelt of mild disinfectant. Curtains flanked picture windows that looked out onto a native garden. A handful of residents chatted while others had vacant looks on their faces. A pleasant enough place, Jill thought. A John Wayne re-run was playing on the television and a nurse was pushing a trolley, dispensing medication. She smiled at the wrinkled faces. They all had that disappointed, exhausted look of old age, of regret and acceptance of what their lives had become.

Jill asked at reception for Maureen Hardcastle. The woman was about to point her out when a stooped, bony man with big ears shuffled past. 'Maureen's over there, by the window — she's the pretty one.'

'Thanks.' Jill gave him a nod and headed toward Maureen.

'You must be from the police,' Maureen said when Jill walked up to her.

Jill looked into the woman's eyes; the rims were red, the irises almost colourless. 'Yes, that's right, my name is Detective Jill Brennan. I wanted to ask you about Robbie and Fin Calloway and their grandmother, Grace Calloway.'

'You don't look like the police. You're too young.'

Jill smiled and flashed her ID. Lucky she hadn't been officially suspended; otherwise she wouldn't even have her ID to fall back on. Maureen put on a pair of reading glasses and examined Jill's warrant card. She considered the likeness and said her hair looked nice in a ponytail.

'Do you mind if I ask you a few questions?' Jill asked.

'You'll have to be quick about it; I'm about to have my lunch. We're having roast lamb, today.'

Jill moved Maureen's walker to one side and sat down next to her. 'I wanted to ask what you remember about Robbie and Fin Calloway.' Jill raised her voice. 'They lived next door to you when they were growing up.'

'There's no need to shout, dear. I'm old, not deaf.'

Jill apologised and decided she liked the woman.

'You want to know about Robbie and Fin, you said? They aren't in any trouble are they?'

'No, I just have some routine questions.' Jill thought it was best not to mention Robbie's death in case she upset the woman before she extracted any information from her.

'So, do you remember Robbie and Fin?' Jill looked at Maureen Hardcastle and wondered how reliable her memory was.

'There are some people you never forget.' Maureen looked off into the distance and Jill took her hand, thinking it would return her to the present. She pressed her arthritic fingers. They were cold.

'The children came to live with Gracie after their parents died in that horrible car accident. You shouldn't blame her, you know.' Maureen pursed her pale, thin lips.

'Gracie?'

Maureen nodded.

'Shouldn't blame Gracie for what?'

'It was a hard decision to make, but she couldn't do it to her son he…' She stopped herself short.

Jill looked into the woman's eyes. 'What decision did Gracie have to make?'

'Oh, I can't tell you that, dear. I promised Gracie I would never tell another living soul. I will take her secret to the grave.'

'But this could be important.' Jill leaned forward. 'Can't you tell me anything? It's for Fin…she's not well.'

The woman seemed to be studying her. 'It was Patrick he…'

'Patrick?'

'Yes dear, Patrick. He was Gracie's son, from her first marriage. He left around the time Fin was fourteen.'

'You coming to lunch, Maureen?' said the man with the big ears.

'You go along; I'll be there shortly. Poor man, he's lost his marbles,' Maureen whispered.

Jill smiled but knew she had to wrap this conversation up quickly before Maureen was reminded again of her lamb roast lunch. 'Tell me more about this Patrick.'

'I'm sorry, dear I've already said too much.' Maureen grabbed the side of the armchair and stood up. 'We're having roast lamb today, you know.' She struggled to reach her walker. 'Oh, but I told you that already, didn't I? Yes, I'm sure I did.'

Jill got to her feet and helped Maureen with her walker. 'But Gracie Calloway is dead, surely you can tell me, now.'

'I'm not the type to betray a friend, even if she is dead.'

'But —'

Maureen Hardcastle waved her finger at Jill. 'A promise is a promise.'

Jill walked with Maureen to the dining room in the far wing. The smell of lamb and baked potatoes spread down the corridor. 'I can't talk to you anymore, my lunch will be getting cold.'

'Just one more question.' Jill looked over at the woman from reception who she'd spoken to earlier. She had a scowl on her face and was headed their way.

'Maureen, what were Robbie and Fin like as children? Did they ever get into any trouble?'

'Robbie was a good kid, but Fin, she was strange. Sitting up in that Jacaranda tree in Gracie's backyard, all day, playing those silly games of hers. She fell out of that tree once, you know, landed on her head.' Maureen laughed. 'I don't think she was ever the same after that. She was always going on about castles and towers and the like, wanted everyone to call her princess.'

'Maureen, there you are my precious.' 'Big Ears' was waiting for Maureen by the door to the dining room. Nothing was standing between Maureen and her routine.


The beams from the car headlights bounced off the wet road in front of her. Jill turned on the fog lights and pushed on through the tangle of traffic on the motorway, convinced Robbie's death had something to do with Grace Calloway's secret. Maureen Hardcastle would clearly do anything to protect that secret. Unless old age was working on her mind, which meant it was something big, a secret worth protecting at all costs. Jill wondered what she could do to convince her to talk.

Jill arrived home around five o'clock. She grabbed a bottle of wine from the refrigerator, unscrewed the cap and poured herself a glass. She walked over to the dining table, sat down and opened up her laptop. Her mind went immediately to her conversation with Maureen Hardcastle. Jill decided to check out the birth, deaths and marriages register. Maureen had mentioned the name Patrick, and Jill knew from her training that sometimes the person who found the body was the person responsible for the death. So she started with Patrick Hill. Was it possible the Patrick Maureen spoke of could be Patrick Hill?

It didn't take long to confirm her suspicion. Jill put her hands behind her head and sat back in her chair. Patrick Hill was the same Patrick Maureen knew...Gracie's son from a first marriage, which made him Fin and Robbie's half-uncle. He'd changed his family name from Reilly to Hill around the time he left Katoomba. If Robbie had ever tried to find Patrick he would have been searching for Patrick Reilly not Patrick Hill. So, if nothing else, there was a family connection between the two men. Now why wouldn't Patrick mention that to the police? She recorded relevant dates, including the date Patrick was born. Next, she searched Robbie's birth details. Now, it all made sense. Why hadn't she thought to look for this information before? She couldn't wait to tell Rimis about the connection. She picked up her phone but then changed her mind. She'd need more proof. So what if Robbie and Patrick Hill were related that didn't mean anything. Or did it? Jill checked her watch. It wasn't too late. She grabbed her phone and dialled the Burlington Aged Care Home. This time she wouldn't let Maureen Hardcastle sideline her. She sat back in her chair and waited for her call to be answered.

# THIRTY-TWO

FIN PARKED HER CAR ON Balmain Road and made her
way on foot to Callan Park, clutching a bunch of
flowers. The sun has been out earlier but now grey
clouds hung overhead, an obvious sign rain was on its
way — again. She walked through the grounds, stopping occasionally to look at the details of a particular
building or the signs, like the one that told her the
building in front of her was Ward 18. She wondered
what had gone on inside the ward and in all the other
abandoned buildings scattered around the place now
left to rot. If it were another time, she would have been
sent to a place like this and then, like many others,
would have been conveniently forgotten.

A light, rain-filled breeze drifted in from Iron Cove
and caressed her cheeks. She caught a scent of perfume
from the flowers she was carrying. A man in a striped
shirt striding out in front of his dog smiled at her when
he walked past. She shoved her free hand in the pocket
of her coat and walked a little faster.

She spun around, her head buzzed, the landscape a
blur; tree-lined avenues, bitumen paths, blocks of
sandstone — primitive and raw, a dog, its tongue
trailing from its mouth, a gravel car park, cars parked at
odd angles, cracked muddy puddles now the rain had
stopped and the sun was out.

Her feet followed the familiar path and when she
reached the tower, her heart sank. The tower was
stained grey from the recent rain and Fin tried to

imagine from what point Robbie jumped, and then followed the trajectory to where he might have landed. The tears came. How had it come to this? When had it started? With her drinking? Or did it go further back than that to when her parents had died? Or was it when Uncle Patrick started to look at her differently? She knelt and laid the flowers by the door. She noticed the brass lock, which had already been replaced. And someone had nailed a sign to the door. It said: Danger, Keep out.

Fin drove onto the M4. It was usually a ninety-minute drive to the Blue Mountains but with the traffic the way it was, it was going to take longer. She wouldn't arrive now until after dark.

The sound of the wipers snapping back and forth on the windscreen reminded her of a metronome. The piano lessons she'd been forced to take as a child had been a waste of time. She'd been more interested in the polished timber pyramid box and the regular ticking of the steel pointer, than the ivory keys at her fingertips.

She shifted gears and took her foot off the accelerator. She'd been making excellent time up until now. The traffic inched forward. Police sirens screamed up ahead. She fumbled inside her bag and found a pack of cigarettes — only two left. She wound down the window and lit up.

The driver of the car in front of her got out and stood in the middle of the road with his hands on his hips and stared into the distance. She watched him through the windscreen, flicked ash out of the window and thought of Robbie. Death, like a thief, crept up on you when you least expected it.

Fifteen minutes later, the traffic began to move. Fin saw the reason for the holdup. A minor collision between a white delivery truck and a family sedan. Fin had smoked the last of her cigarettes; looked at the road sign that said the next turn-off was five kilometres up ahead. She took the exit, drove through heavy fog and pulled up outside the Lapstone Hotel.

A cosy fire in the sports bar of the Hotel crackled and glowed in the stone fireplace. On her way to the bar, Fin walked past a few old-timers on vinyl bar stools. The barman asked what he could get her. She ordered two whiskey shots and a pack of cigarettes. While she waited, she noticed a group of men playing pool in the room behind the bar. A sharp ceramic click-click signalled a fresh break on the pool table. Their laughter irritated her.

After she'd paid for the drinks and cigarettes, she took a seat at a table close enough to the fire to feel its warmth. She swallowed the first mouthful of whiskey. It burned her throat. She swallowed again; felt the warmth spread through her body.

The man at the next table stared at her. Spidery, purple lines ran up his cheeks — the signs of a heavy drinker. He pushed his chair back, walked to the bar, and a few minutes later returned with a schooner of frothy beer. He winked at her. 'Filthy weather, isn't it?' he said. 'They reckon it will snow before the weekend.' He took a gulp of his beer. 'So love, you staying the night?'

Fin noticed his stubby nicotine-stained fingers, the gravelly tone of his voice — everything about him irritated her. She didn't reply straight away. Instead, she looked at the door. 'I have to get going.' She gathered her cigarettes and lighter from the table. He was still staring at her. Fin had seen that look before and wondered if she had said or done something to offend him or had encouraged him in some way. With Robbie gone, she would have to be careful what she said to men and the way she behaved in front of them.

Fin rushed back to her car and started the engine. She shivered, turned the heater up and looked back at the hotel. She half expected the man to rush out and try to get in the car beside her. She threw her cigarettes into her bag and backed out of the car space in a hurry.

An hour later Fin walked up to the check-in desk in the wood-panelled reception area of the Katoomba Hotel and asked about her booking. While she waited for her room key, she stood in front of the open fire to warm herself. She rubbed her hands together and realised any visitor to the Blue Mountains would expect the warmth and ambience of such a fire.

Once she had her key, she took the two flights of carpeted stairs to her room. The room had cost sixty dollars for the night and for budget accommodation it was clean and cosy, but didn't have its own bathroom. A shared bathroom was located down the hall.

The bed looked comfortable enough and she threw her carry-all down on it and began to unpack her pyjamas and toiletry bag. She would have stayed at her grandmother's house but the gas had already been disconnected and without the gas heaters she would have frozen to death.

The only window in the hotel room looked out on-to an empty car park, and beyond that she could make out the rear of an Italian restaurant, a pet store and a laundromat. She couldn't see the mountains, but if she'd wanted a view she would have gone somewhere more upmarket. Besides, she wasn't here for the sights;

she was here to speak to the real estate agent about selling her grandmother's house and to finish sorting her grandmother's possessions. She and Robbie had planned to do it together. Now it was up to her.

# THIRTY-THREE

Jill dialled Rimis's mobile number. 'Boss, it's me.'

'What are you doing ringing me? You're on leave. You're supposed to be getting your head together.'

'I drove to Katoomba today,' Jill said.

'That's good to hear, the Blue Mountains are nice this time of year.'

'While I was there I paid a visit to Grace Calloway's neighbour. She remembered Robbie and Fin from when they were kids.'

'I can't believe I'm hearing this.'

'Grace Calloway had a son from a previous marriage.'

'Brennan, this is all very interesting but —'

'You'll never guess who the son was?' Jill didn't wait for Rimis to answer. 'Patrick Hill,' she said.

Silence. Then, 'Go on.'

At last, she had his attention. 'I told you Grace Calloway died recently. I'm trying to track down her solicitor to find out what was in her will, who the beneficiaries were and what sort of estate she left. I'm guessing the beneficiaries were Robbie and Fin. According to Maureen Hardcastle —'

'Who the bloody hell is Maureen Hardcastle?'

'She's the ex-neighbour. I went to visit her. She lives in a nursing home in Katoomba. She was a bit cagey at first, wouldn't let on too much about the family and said Grace Calloway had made her promise to keep the family secrets. When I got home and made the Patrick Hill connection I rang the nursing home and got her to talk.'

'And how did you manage that? Or shouldn't I ask.'

'You don't need to know the details, but let's just say she was willing to tell me everything she knew after I had a few stern words with her.'

'So, what was the Calloway family secret?' Rimis asked.

'Patrick Hill sexually abused Fin when she was a child. He was also the driver of the car that killed Fin and Robbie's parents. Grace covered up for him and he was never charged. When he moved away from Katoomba he changed his name from Reilly to Hill. For obvious reasons he didn't want Robbie or Fin to find him, or anyone else for that matter.'

Silence.

'You there, boss?'

'Yeah, I'm here. I was thinking.'

'Robbie's death has something to do with Patrick Hill. I'm certain of it. This could explain why Robbie moved to Glover Street. Somehow he finds out where Patrick is living and practically moves in next-door. And then who finds Robbie's body in Callan Park?'

'Patrick Hill,' Rimis said.

'Exactly.'

'I think we might need to pay Mr Hill a visit. Why don't you come into the station tomorrow? You and Rawlings can go and see him together. I don't want you going on your own.'

'Okay. I'll come in early, it will be a good chance to clear my in-tray before we go to see Patrick Hill.' Jill ended the call and punched the air with her fist.

# THIRTY-FOUR

IT WAS 6.30 am. Jill found a parking space in the station car park and was about to turn the engine off when she saw Rimis running towards her. She pressed the passenger window release button.

'What is it?' she asked.

Rimis got into the passenger seat and yanked at his seatbelt. 'Drive.'

'Where are we going?' Jill put the car into reverse, sending droplets of dew dribbling down the windscreen.

'Callan Park.' Rimis folded his arms across his chest.

'What's happened?' Jill drove out of the station car park, slamming Rimis back into the seat and headrest, siren and lights flashing. She flicked the indicator on and turned left at the traffic lights on Archer Street and headed towards Mowbray Road.

Rimis gave her a sideward glance. 'There's just been a call to triple zero. A kid's found a body by the tower at Callan Park. It's Patrick Hill.'


A film of mist hung over the same car park Jill had driven into the night Robbie had died. With the pre-dawn light barely visible she pulled up behind a patrol car with its flashers on. A uniformed officer got out of the car ahead and walked up to the driver's side. It was Constable Patullo. Jill powered down the window.

'A bit like Groundhog Day isn't it?' Patullo said.

Rimis leaned over and said. 'What have we got?'

Patullo wiped a drip from the end of his nose. 'A kid on his way to work decided to take a shortcut. I bet he wishes he didn't now. He's in shock. The ambulance isn't far away.'

Rimis and Brennan unbuckled their seat belts, got out of the car and followed Patullo to the patrol car. Patullo opened the rear passenger door. The boy got out. He was wearing a plastic rain poncho, the type available at any discount store. There was an intense smell of rain, wet plastic and fear about him.

The music from his headphones was so loud Rimis grabbed them and pulled them from his ears. The boy was jabbering, not making much sense.

'Slow down, son,' Rimis said to him. 'Just calm yourself, take a deep breath and then you can tell me your name and what this is all about.'

He couldn't be more than sixteen, Jill thought.

'My name's Jordan Brandt.'

'You made the emergency call, Jordan?'

'Yeah. There's a freakin' dead body over there by the tower. He's just sitting there, man. I thought he was asleep, but he didn't look right. I called out to him, but he didn't answer me. I went over to him to ask if he needed help. That's when I saw the hole in his head.'

'What time did you find him?' Rimis asked.

Jordan took his phone from his pocket and checked the time. His hand was shaking. 'About fifteen minutes ago.'

'Did you phone anybody else? Take photos?' Jill asked.

'No I didn't take photos. And I only called my mum.'

'Give me your phone. I don't want you making any more calls or texting your friends,' Jill said. 'Or posting anything on Facebook or Twitter.'

'Did you touch him?' Rimis asked.

'What?'

'Did you touch him?'

'No, of course I didn't. I knew there was nothing I could do.' The boy's nose was dripping. 'I watch CSI. I know you're not supposed to contaminate the crime scene.'

Jill noticed the look on Rimis's face. He wanted to smile but didn't.

'What were you doing here, anyway?' Jill asked.

'It's a short cut. I can save myself ten minutes if I cut through the park. I catch the bus on Balmain Road to the city. I've got a part-time job at the Four Seasons Hotel. I'm a kitchen hand there and I should be at work now. I'm going to get the sack, I just know it.'

'You'll have to wait here,' Rimis said. 'We'll have more questions for you later. And we'll need a statement from you.'

Jill watched Rimis as he took control of the scene. Back up and the ambulance had arrived and the uniforms were cordoning off the area with police tape.

'You okay, Jordan?' Jill asked him.

The boy returned his earplugs to his ears and pulled up his hoodie. 'What do you think, lady? I just found a dead body, didn't I?'

# THIRTY-FIVE

RIMIS TURNED UP THE COLLAR of his jacket and with Brennan by his side they made their way across the frost-whitened grass to the tower. They recognised the victim immediately.

'A coincidence?'

'Seems unlikely,' Rimis said.

Patrick Hill was in a sitting position with his back against the wall next to the tower door. His head lolled against his chest, his thin legs splayed out in front of him. He was soaked through; his hair plastered flat to his skull, a yellow beanie lay on the ground next to him. Rimis blew into his hands. When he looked up he saw Greer Ross striding towards them.

'What is it about this place?' Doctor Ross called. 'Two deaths in the same location, less than a week apart?'

Rimis and Brennan stepped aside to make room for Doctor Ross to examine the body.

'You didn't waste any time getting here,' Rimis said.

'I was already in the car on my way to work when I got the call.'

Rimis thought Patrick Hill could have been asleep if it wasn't for his ashen pallor and the bullet hole between the eyes.

Greer began her examination. 'No powder burns, absence of stippling. He was shot at close range, possibly post-mortem.'

'Post-mortem?'

Doctor Ross gave a nod to Rimis. 'Doesn't appear to be any bleeding from the head wound. I won't know for sure if it occurred post-mortem until I open him up, but at this stage it looks that way.' She examined the back of his head. 'No exit wound. The skull feels intact, the scalp unbroken.' She continued her external examination.

Rimis's hand cupped his chin. He looked down at Patrick Hill. 'I think the body was staged. What do you think, Greer?'

Brennan looked at Rimis. She'd never heard him call Doctor Ross by her first name.

'Give me a minute, Nick. Let me catch my breath and gather my thoughts.'

And she called him, Nick, not Inspector. Jill looked at them both and wondered if there was something going on between them.

There was a moment of silence.

'I think you're right. The body is too symmetrical,' Greer said.

Rimis shuffled his feet and crossed his arms, watching while Greer pulled up the legs of Patrick Hill's tracksuit.

'What is it?' Rimis asked.

'Dependent lividity. The lower part of his body is mottled from blood pooling. Take a look.' She pointed to Hill's legs.

'So he died in that position.'

'Looks like it. I'll know more when I get him on the table.' Greer peered into Patrick Hill's mouth. 'What's this?' She picked out a white feather with the tips of her gloved fingers.

Brennan pulled out a plastic evidence bag from her pocket. 'Boss, it looks like the same type of feather Phil Hammond found in the tower the night Robbie died.'

'Where the hell is the police photographer?' Greer snapped. 'He should have been here by now. We need photos.'

Rimis looked at his watch. 'Peak hour.'

Fifteen minutes later, the police photographer arrived. 'Sorry, guys, the traffic's a nightmare.' He walked around the body, careful not to contaminate the scene before he crouched down and took a close-up shot of Patrick Hill's face.

'The media are going to have a field day once they catch wind of this, if they haven't already,' Rimis said.

'I was rostered on to do Robbie's autopsy this morning…until I got your call. I'll see if I can have Patrick Hill put on the priority list. And before you ask me, time of death, best guess, between seven and midnight last night based on rigor and body temp.'

Rimis looked at Brennan. 'Didn't he normally walk his dog around nine-thirty?'

'Yep,' Jill said. 'Speaking of Brian, isn't that him over there?'

Everyone turned around.

'Brennan, go and fetch the dog will you?'

'But, boss, I'm not really a dog person, I —'

'Brennan, get the dog.'

Brian was about twenty metres away. He'd just popped his head up from a thick hedge of ivy and barked, as if on cue. When Jill walked over to him he was on his belly, paws outstretched in front of him. His white coat was covered in a thick layer of mud. Brennan untangled his lead. Brian stood up, wagged his tail and licked her hand.

'What are we going to do with him?' Jill said when she walked back to Rimis.

'Go and talk to Mr Hill's neighbour, take Brian with you. Maybe the neighbour will take the dog or at least look after him for the time being. We need to get a hold of Fin Calloway. She'd be his next of kin I'm guessing.'

'If only Brian could speak, we'd have two deaths solved by now,' Jill said before she walked off and left Rimis and Greer Ross to it.


Rimis checked to see if anybody was listening before he caught Greer gently by the arm. It was the lightest of touches. 'Look, Greer, I wanted to speak to you about...what happened between us. I...'

'It's all right, Nick you don't have to say anything.'

'I want to apologise for taking off the way I did. I guess I panicked.'

'Nick, I had a bad day, you had a bad day. It's all back to business now, right?'

Rimis thought he heard a hint of regret in her voice. Regret for what they'd shared, or regret that it would never be repeated?

'I'll let you know if we can prioritise the autopsies.' She gave him a smile and turned away.

Rimis watched her walk back towards the car park. Perhaps he was taking what had happened between them too seriously. What would be the harm in seeing her again?

About five minutes later Patrick Hill's body was taken away.

# THIRTY-SIX

FIN RUBBED HER FACE AND pressed her fingers against her eyelids. She had to think for a moment before she remembered where she was. Katoomba. Today she was going to finish packing the last of Gracie's possessions then she'd go and speak to one of the local real estate agents about selling the house. She'd pestered Robbie to do something about selling the house at Gracie's funeral but he'd said he was busy and couldn't afford the time. Busy with what?

The curtains were drawn but through the cracks she could tell it was morning. Fin checked her watch — 6.30 am. She threw back the bedclothes, took a deep breath and tried to steady her heartbeat. Something wasn't right. She looked at what she was wearing. Why was she still dressed in last night's clothes? She looked across at her shoes by the bedroom door — wet and muddied. Something's wrong. Something bad has happened.

Fin got out of bed and caught herself in the full-length mirror on the oak wardrobe. Mascara smears trailed across her cheeks. Her face was pale and drawn. Where had she been last night? She grabbed her handbag from the bedside table. Her purse was still there and so were her credit cards and a fifty-dollar note. She searched for her phone and found it under her pillow. She had three missed calls. No caller ID for any of them. She checked her voicemail.

Adam had left a message at eleven-twenty last night. He was shouting. 'What the fuck is wrong with you, Fin? I can't believe what just happened. Just stay away from me. Don't phone me and don't come around to the restaurant looking for me. For Christ's sake, you have to stop drinking. It's caused enough trouble.'

What trouble? Was he talking about her losing her job? Or something else? Robbie had been worried about her drinking and blackouts, too. Fin didn't think she'd been drinking that much, at least not enough to cause her to blackout. Where was she last night? What had she done? She sank back onto the bed and looked up at the ceiling.

She had no memory of the night Robbie died, either. What if she'd been there? Maybe they had a fight. Could she have pushed him? Bile rose and she forced it back down again. She remembered the wet and muddy clothes on the floor when the police had come to her apartment. Once again her muddy shoes told a story, but what? The last thing she remembered was driving down the highway to the Alexandria Hotel, about an hour after she'd checked in. She'd suddenly had to escape the confines of her room. At the Alexandria, a live band had been playing. She'd a few drinks and...

Fin walked up the steps to the front door of Robbie's cottage and unlocked the door with her spare key. She sat down on the sofa and looked around the sitting room.

It was dark outside. She checked the breech of Robbie's gun, tucked it into the waistband of her jeans. She didn't know how she'd got Robbie's gun from the metal box where he kept it, but she'd found it in her bedside drawer the morning after his death and she'd been hiding it ever since. Robbie had brought the gun home after work to use on Patrick Hill to show him Robbie meant business.

Fin turned the television set on, sat down on the sofa and waited.

The alarm beeped on her watch. It was time to go. She locked the cottage, crossed the park and walked towards the clock tower. She thought it strange that the clock tower had been built without a clock; perhaps the patients hadn't wanted to be reminded of lost time.

Fin followed the path through to the courtyard and stood in the shadows. A dog barked and she knew Patrick Hill was close. She reached into her backpack and removed a small, wispy feather from a box. She held it tightly between her fingertips.

'It's a terrible night to be out,' Patrick Hill said.

The leaves on the nearby trees shook on their branches. A quarter moon was rising and she could just make out his features. She wanted to run at him, end it now, but she'd waited for this moment for too long, planned everything so perfectly, to ruin it now by her impatience.

'I want to talk to you, Fin. Set it right between us,' Patrick said. 'It's been a long time since I saw you. I think you were fourteen when I left. You probably don't believe me, but I'm sorry.'

Sorry? Is that all you can say? After what you did to my family and me.

'You must think I ruined your life. And if I was in any way responsible for what happened to Robbie, I promise I'll make it up to you.'

Fin was silent. How could he possibly make up for the loss of her family?

'It's too late for Robbie, but not for you. With the money you'll get from your grandmother's and Robbie's estates, I can help you invest it. I wanted to talk to you about some ideas I've got.'

Fin didn't answer. She didn't want to spoil the surprise she had waiting for him.

'I want to try to set things right between us.' He shifted from foot to foot. 'I've been thinking a lot about it lately, especially now Robbie's gone,' he said. 'I think we can be family again, just like the old days.'

The old days? Fin shuddered.

'The key,' Fin said in a voice that was not her own. She pulled the hood of her navy rain jacket further down over her eyes.

Patrick searched for the key on his key ring. 'Here it is.' His hand shook when he handed it to her.

'Can't we talk here?' Patrick asked. 'Why do we have to go up the tower? I'm not a young man.'

Fin didn't reply. The key turned smoothly in the lock; she handed the keys back to him and pushed against the door.

'Wait,' he said.

Fin ignored him and started climbing the stairs. Stopped.

'Fin, wait. Please.'

She hesitated, but then heard his footsteps behind. When she reached the top, she pulled out Robbie's gun and ran the palm of her hand over the dull plastic grip. A shudder ran through her, which had nothing to do with the sharp wind blowing through the arches.

Patrick took the last of the steps, his breathing laboured. Fin raised the gun and pointed it at him. He froze.

'Everything looks perfectly normal from here, doesn't it, Uncle Patrick? Look out there. Everybody going about their business. Nobody has any idea you're about to die. Within about two minutes, I reckon.'

Patrick took a step towards her. 'What the hell are you up to?'

Fin ignored him. 'If Robbie hadn't found out you'd changed your name to Hill and were on a paedophile watch list, you wouldn't be standing here, and neither would I.'

There was confusion and fear in Patrick's eyes. Fin pulled the hood back from her face. She took a step back from him and aimed the gun at the middle of his forehead.

'For Christ's sake, Fin, is this your idea of some sick joke?'

'It's no joke.' Fin laughed. 'I'm fucking serious.'

'Put the gun down. Let's talk. I'm sure we can fix whatever's worrying you.'

'What's worrying me! As if you don't know. Shut up. I don't want to hear anything you have to say. You ruined my life; ruined Robbie's life and you killed my parents. And now, it's time for you to die. To finally pay.'

'Fin, I'm sorry. I was weak, I never meant to; it was the drink.' Patrick held his hands out to her, palms facing up.

'Shut up, you sick bastard.' She waved the gun at him. 'Gracie told Robbie everything before she died. Told him you were driving the night of the car accident. How you were drunk and drove our parents' car off the road. Gracie covered for you because she didn't want you to go to prison.'

'Let me explain. Please, Fin.'

'It's too late for explanations.'

Patrick gasped for air, held his chest with one hand. He stepped backwards, tripped, leaned up against the wall, head bowed. He tried to stand upright, but didn't have the strength after climbing the stairs.

Fin maintained her position — feet apart just like Robbie had shown her — but her hands were shaking.

'Why are you doing this?' Patrick's voice was weak. 'I'll give you money. You can go away, make a new life for yourself. There's no need to kill me.'

Fin stared at Patrick then looked down at the gun. Wasn't this what Robbie wanted? Compensation for the pain Patrick had caused?

'The money from Robbie's and Gracie's estates and Robbie's life insurance policy will be more than enough. I don't need your filthy money.'

'What about the police, then? That woman detective, she'll work out what you're up to.'

Fin didn't answer him.

Patrick slipped to the ground. Had he fainted? Died? Or maybe he was faking it. It was too dark to tell. She kept the gun out and walked slowly toward him. Once she was close enough, she jabbed him with her foot. He let out a little groan. He looked so pathetic, slumped across the uneven brickwork.

She hadn't planned for this. She tucked the gun into her waistband and put two fingers on his neck. His pulse was weak, but he was still alive. Maybe he'd had a heart attack. He sure had been puffing at the top of the stairs, and then she'd pulled the gun.

She kicked him. He moaned and his lips moved, at first soundlessly and then she could make out her name. Was it to hear his dying confession? Fin wasn't interested; she had to get him to his feet. She checked her watch. Adam would be here soon.

'Come on, get up.' She wrapped his limp arm around her neck and an arm around his waist. His eyes were half-closed. Fin whispered, 'If you can get downstairs, I'll call an ambulance. I promise.' Fin looked at her watch. With each passing second her heart was beating faster, pumping with adrenaline. He wasn't fighting her now, the promise of calling an ambulance did the trick.

After they took the last step, Fin guided him through the door and leaned him against the tower wall. He collapsed from the effort and Fin managed to ease him down the wall so he was in a sitting position with his legs splayed open. After a few seconds he opened his eyes and gave a rattled groan before his eyes fluttered shut and his head slumped forward.

Fin felt for a pulse. Patrick Hill was dead.

She reached into her coat pocket and pulled out a white feather. She looked at it for a moment. 'Coward.' Fin opened Patrick's mouth and slipped the feather onto his tongue. She stared down at his limp body. It was done now, finished with. She searched Patrick's pockets for his wallet. If she took that, maybe the police would think it was a robbery gone wrong. She found it and tucked it into the pocket of her rain jacket. Fin wondered what she should do next. She hadn't thought beyond this moment.


Adam Lee entered the courtyard by the eastern entrance avoiding the CCTV cameras, the way Fin had told him to. He turned on the flashlight app on his phone and saw Fin standing by the tower. She was looking down at a lump on the ground. It was only when he got closer that he realised it was a body.

'Adam?'

He walked up to her and saw that it was Patrick Hill. 'What's happened to him?'

'He's dead. I only meant to frighten him, I didn't think he would have a heart attack and die on me.'

'Stupid bitch! Give me the gun and get out of here. I'm sick of tidying up your messes.'


Fin pushed herself off the bed. Nagging pangs of hunger played havoc with her stomach. Had she eaten last night? If she forced herself to eat something maybe the waves of nausea would pass. She changed her clothes without showering and went downstairs to the hotel's restaurant. She didn't have much time. It was a ten-minute drive to Gracie's house. If she worked steadily she would back in Sydney by late afternoon. She didn't want to stay in the Mountains another night.

She stood at the top of the stairs and looked down. She felt dizzy again. She wanted to lie down but she knew she had to eat and get over to Gracie's house. The Salvation Army was coming at nine to collect the last of Gracie's furniture. Fin had kept a couple of things aside, thinking she might make room for them in her apartment, but there were too many memories.

Fin joined the handful of people eating breakfast early. A large, energetic woman who Fin took to be the proprietor dashed to and fro between the kitchen and the reception desk, stopping to chat and joke with the guests. She gave Fin a quick smile and said hello when she walked past her table. The warmth from the open fire did nothing to ease the fear or Fin's thumping headache. She looked around the room. Her eyes settled on the couple at the next table. Fin looked at him, ignored her. He reminded Fin of Robbie, that particular way he had of spooning his cereal into his mouth and the way he tilted his head to one side when he laughed.

Fin blinked hard. Robbie was gone. She dug her nails into her palms, while tears stung her cheeks. She distracted herself by looking at the walls covered in subdued wallpaper and the timber table, which was sticky and thickly lacquered. It wasn't like the pub she'd stopped at in Lapstone. There were no poker machines or pool tables, no posters advertising Tuesday steak nights or trivia nights. She studied the breakfast menu and decided on eggs and toast.

A waiter poured coffee into her cup. He put a jug of milk and sachets of sugar down on the table, smiled at her but she didn't smile back — she didn't know why she should. She looked around the room and then fixed on the television. Video footage of Callan Park was on the screen. Someone turned the sound up. Ticker information scrolling the bottom of the screen caught her attention as much as the pictures being shown of the clock tower. 'Another death at Callan Park.' The words scrolled on and she listened to the news announcer. 'Patrick Hill,' he was saying, 'the dog walker who found the body of a police officer in Callan Park a week ago, was found dead early this morning in the grounds of Callan Park. He was discovered by a teenager on his way to work…'

# THIRTY-SEVEN

JILL LOOKED DOWN AT BRIAN. 'Come on, boy.' She took a few steps, making her way across the park to speak to Patrick Hill's neighbour, but then stopped. She wanted to speak to Jordan first. She double-backed to the patrol car. He was in the back seat, his mother by his side. They got out of the car. Jill introduced herself and was about to question Jordan more when she changed her mind. The boy was shaking and clearly in no state to talk. She arranged a time for him and his mother to come into the station tomorrow to give a formal statement.

The woman wrapped her arms around her son and they walked away. Jill tried to imagine her own mother but time blurred memories. She had photos of her, of course, and her father had talked about how kind and funny she was, but with her father dead there was nobody to share her memories. Even memories of her father were beginning to fade. They were slipping away and she could no longer hold onto them.

She sighed. 'Let's go, Brian.' She pulled on the lead and headed across the park to Glover Street. They both could do with a walk. The ground was water-logged but at least the rain had stopped.

Jill stood at the front door of Patrick Hill's neighbour's cottage and rang the doorbell. Brian was jumping up on his hind legs, scratching at the door. Jill tugged at the lead and pulled him away.

The cottage was similar in style and age to the cottage next door and while she waited for the door to be answered, she looked around and noticed the well-kept garden. When she rang the doorbell again, the door opened. The woman was in her dressing gown.

'Brian. Just look at you, what have you been up to?'

The dog pulled away from Jill and bounded off down the hall, sliding across the polished timber floorboards as he raced towards the back of the house.

Jill showed her ID. 'Detective Brennan from Chatswood Police.'

'Goodness, what is it? Has something happened to Mr Hill?'

'Why would you ask that?'

'Well, after that poor policemen killed himself the other day, we've all been on edge.'

Jill knew the neighbour would find out sooner or later. 'Yes, I'm afraid Mr Hill is dead.'

'Oh my dear Lord. Come in dear, you look half frozen. I'll make us a nice cup of coffee.'

Jill set about removing her wet rain jacket and muddy boots then followed the woman down the hall into a large family room at the rear. The smell of coffee and toast reminded Jill she'd skipped breakfast. The woman put on the kettle, and while she waited for it to boil she picked up Brian; she didn't seem to mind the dog was covered in mud. She stroked his back gently with her bony fingers and his pink skin showed through the fur.

'It was his heart wasn't it? I warned him.'

Jill didn't respond.

'I knew it would be his heart that got him in the end. It was the shock of finding that poor policeman in the park the other night. I've never seen Mr Hill so agitated. He was an old-fashioned type, not the sort of man to show emotion. Not like nowadays where everyone from pollies to footballers ball their eyes out on the telly at the drop of a hat.'

Jill gave a nod. 'What sort of man was he apart from being old-fashioned?'

The woman put Brian down on the floor. 'Well dear, I don't like to speak ill of the dead, but I did have my suspicions about him.' The kettle had boiled and the woman busied herself making two coffees.

'What sort of suspicions?'

The woman turned around, raised her eyebrows. 'Drugs!'

'Really?' Hill wasn't the typical drug-type.

The woman nodded and then loaded a tray with the coffees, milk, sugar and a plate of salt crackers. She led Jill through to the living room and they sat down on the sofa.

Jill poured milk into her coffee. 'What makes you think Mr Hill was involved in drugs?'

'It was all the comings and goings. I knew it had to be drugs. What else could it have been?' She picked up the plate of crackers. 'Would you like one dear?'

Jill waved her hand. 'No, thanks. Tell me more about these comings and goings?'

'Asians.' The woman slurped her tea.

'Asians?'

'Yes, they'd pull up in their cars. Turn the engine off and wait. Then they'd go in. Sometimes they had children with them. I was outraged. Those children should have been in bed.'

'So, how often did you see them?' Jill asked.

'Not very often, maybe once a month.' She took another sip of coffee and stared out the window.

'Was there anything else?' Jill asked.

A pause, then, 'Well, there was the night the policeman died. I just happened to be closing the curtains when I saw one of them. He was waiting like the rest, except he didn't go next door to Mr Hill's. I saw him get out of his car and walk off towards Callan Park.'

# THIRTY-EIGHT

RIMIS PARKED ON ARUNDEL STREET and walked into the Glebe Morgue. He didn't recognise the woman behind the glass but he figured even morgue receptionists had to take leave at some point.

He held up his ID and was buzzed through security. 'I'm here to see Doctor Ross,' he said. He signed the blue visitor's book and headed down the corridor towards the autopsy rooms.

The dead were the dead as far as Rimis was concerned — death was what happened to everyone in the end — but attending autopsies was still the worst part of his job. He walked into the autopsy room, took off his jacket and grabbed a green gown. The room was chilly and smelled of chemicals.

Greer was taking photos but stopped when she saw him. She looked up and greeted him with a nod, a look that said business as usual. 'Where's Detective Brennan? You two seem inseparable.'

Rimis detected a hint of jealousy in her voice. 'I didn't think she needed to be here for this one.'

Greer turned back to the body in front of her. 'I've just started with Robbie Calloway. I shouldn't be more than two hours and then I'll begin on Patrick Hill.'

Rimis had learnt to maintain a stoic front whenever he walked into the autopsy room at the Glebe Morgue. It was the last place he ever wanted to be, but he stood impassive by the table, flinched only once when Doctor Ross stabbed needles into the cadaver and collected vitreous fluid from the eye. How did she do this job? Dealing with the dead every day.

'You feel all right? You're looking…'

'Fine.'

Greer stopped what she was doing and looked at him over her facemask.

Rimis cleared his throat. 'I want to apologise again for the way I walked out on you yesterday morning. I was embarrassed by what had happened given we work together and, to be honest, it's been a while since I… I mean…Oh, shit, help me out here, Greer. You know what I'm trying to say.'

Greer smiled beneath her mask. 'Apology accepted.'

Rimis let out a deep sigh. He focused on the case again, more familiar and comfortable territory. 'So, what can you tell me?' he said.

'Everything so far points to suicide or accidental death. He could have been skylarking, a few drinks too many, hit his head, lost his balance and fallen. When we get the tox reports we'll have a better idea.' Greer reached for the dissection knife and confidently sliced through the torso. She picked up a pair of shears, snapped apart the ribs and lifted off the sternum, releasing the foul odour of blood and offal.

Rimis saw the concentration on her face. 'You look tired.'

'I don't suppose that would have anything to do with me working extra cases.' Greer put down the knife. 'Nick,' she said and removed her splatter shield, 'what happened between us, well, I know it's not going to work. It's better if we're friends. Okay?'

Rimis gave a small nod, but wasn't sure if he was ready to drop it. Doctor Ross got back to work.

After a few moments Rimis said, 'I've never slept with her you know.'

Greer stared at him. 'What?'

'I said, I've never slept with her.'

'Who are you talking about?'

'Brennan.'

Greer frowned. 'Why did you tell me that?'

'Because I thought you should know, in case someone's said anything to you. There's always talk around the station about who's sleeping with who. The truth is, I'm Jill's friend and mentor.'

'Why do you think I'd be the slightest bit interested in who you have or haven't slept with?'

'Because you're a woman and from my experience women are curious about that sort of thing.'

Greer shook her head.

'I can't stop thinking about you,' Rimis said softly. No matter what he did and how many times he'd tried to convince himself otherwise, he couldn't get Greer Ross out of his mind. Maybe this whole idea of not dating women he worked with was bullshit. With the long hours and the type of work policing involved, how else was he going to meet someone who understood his life?

'And why would that be?

'Do you always ask so many questions?'

She met his gaze. 'It's my job to ask questions. Look, Nick, I like you, but we're both professionals doing a difficult job and we need to focus. So I'd really appreciate it if you didn't flirt with me or distract me while I'm working.'

'Message received loud and clear, Doctor Ross.' Rimis saw the slightest twitch of her lips. 'But you must know by now I'm the persistent type. I don't give up easily.' He flashed her a grin and walked towards the door. 'I'm going out for a coffee. I'll be back later.'


An hour and a half after Rimis left the morgue, the gurney carrying Patrick Hill's body was rolled into the autopsy room. Doctor Ross looked at his face; she'd seen worse. It was pale and cold, nothing unusual about it, apart from the bullet wound to the forehead, a single round hole, no external bleeding. Of all parts of the corpse, the face was the most personal. Someone wanted to leave their mark.

The teeth of the forceps clamped down on the prize. 'Ah, got it,' Doctor Ross said just as Rimis walked into the autopsy room.

'Your timing is impeccable, Inspector.' Greer Ross held up a .40 calibre bullet between her gloved fingers. 'The entrance point was right of midline, the bullet proceeded downwards to the right cheek.' She took the bullet to the stainless countertop and dropped it into a kidney bowl; it gave a metallic clang. After she photographed the bullet, Rimis opened a plastic evidence bag, she dropped it in and they both signed it.

Rimis studied the projectile through the plastic. 'I wonder…point four is standard police issue and we're still missing a gun.' He passed it back to Doctor Ross. 'Hollow points do more damage than round points.' The tips of hollow point bullets expand on entering a target to cause more damage and to ensure the bullet stops in the target rather than going through the person and then hitting an innocent bystander.

Doctor Ross cleared her throat. 'No signs of a struggle. No grazes on the knuckles or skin under the fingernails, but I did find something you'll be interested in,' she said. 'When the heart stops beating blood stops flowing and clots soon after. My autopsy confirms what I suspected at the crime scene…I found no evidence of bleeding in the brain or any fresh tissue so Patrick Hill was already dead when he was shot in the head. In fact, the cause of death was Acute Myocardial Infarction.' Greer picked up a dish, the one that contained Patrick Hill's heart. Rimis peered in. 'The coronary vessels were severely and diffusely diseased. A clot was present in the artery to the front wall. That's where the heart attack occurred. And that's what killed him.'

'A heart attack?'

'Yes.'

'That doesn't make sense. You sure about this Greer?' Rimis ran his fingers through his hair.

She raised her eyebrows. 'Of course I'm sure.'

'Any idea how long he was dead before he was shot?'

'I can't give you a precise time, but at least five minutes, no more than fifteen.'

Rimis rubbed his hand along his chin. 'Why would someone want to shoot him when he was clearly dead?'

Rimis looked at Patrick Hill. Rigor mortis had faded since he'd seen him last, and he now lay limp. He stared at him, the puzzle on the table. 'I wonder what images his brain registered before he died. I've often thought how much easier our jobs would be if the brain could be dissected in a way, much like a computer, to produce a screen snapshot of the last thing the vic saw before they died.'

'Interesting idea.'

'If only, huh?' Rimis sighed. 'When can I expect the preliminary reports?'

'If you're lucky, tomorrow, if you're not so lucky, two days. For the toxicology reports, you'll be waiting a while, the lab's running almost a week behind schedule.'

'Let me know when you have them and maybe we can talk about the results over a drink at Otto's.' He gave her a cheeky look and headed for the door before she had time to respond.


Greer had changed out of her scrubs and was at her desk in her office, typing up her initial notes. Her thoughts went to Rimis and their night together. How had an innocent drink after work got so out of hand? A smile played on her lips.

She hadn't gone to Otto's to seek him or anyone else out. She'd simply wanted a drink after a bad day…a very bad day. Then she smiled. There was no denying it; Nick Rimis knew how to make a woman feel special in the bedroom.

Thoughts of Nick Rimis had visited her more than a dozen times since their encounter. But she was embarrassed, knew she'd crossed the line between her professional and personal life. God, what had she been thinking? And she'd told him that she liked it hard…at least she'd said it in Afrikaans. She'd had a dozen or so lovers since her divorce, but Nick was by far the most satisfying. He'd known how to read her every need. What would he be like in bed if he was stone cold sober? Her head filled with images of Nick on top of her, Nick beneath her, Nick inside her. She gave a small shudder and forced herself back to work.

# THIRTY-NINE

JILL KNOCKED ON FIN'S FRONT door. The door opened after the second knock. Fin had a cigarette in hand.

'What are you doing here?' Fin asked. Her voice was raised. She was wearing earphones.

'I wanted to check on you. Make sure you're okay.'

Fin hesitated. 'S'pose you better come in then.'

They moved inside and Jill noticed an overnight bag on the floor. 'You going somewhere?'

Fin raised her head. 'What did you say?'

Jill nodded at the bag.

'Oh, I went to the Blue Mountains. I got back half an hour ago. I had to pack up the last of Gracie's things.' Fin leaned on the back of her sofa. 'Robbie had done most of it over the past couple of weeks.' She took a long drag of her cigarette. 'I wanted to get it finished.'

Jill nodded, but wasn't convinced. 'Where did you stay?' Jill pulled up a stool next to Fin, leaned over and pulled the earphones from Fin's ears. 'I asked where you'd stayed when you were up at the Mountains.'

'The Katoomba Hotel.'

'Is that where you were the whole of last night?'

'Yeah.' Fin narrowed her eyes. 'Want me to show you the hotel receipt?'

'Have you got one?'

While Fin searched her bag, Jill looked at the empty bottles of Johnny Walker by the kitchen sink.

Fin handed her the receipt.

Jill checked the date. 'Mind if I keep this?'

'Go, ahead, I don't want it.'

Jill shoved the receipt into the pocket of her jeans.

Fin stubbed her cigarette and added it to the pile in the saucer. 'So, why are you here, bothering me, again?' Fin glared at Jill. 'Sure doesn't sound like you're just making sure I'm okay.'

'There's been another death at Callan Park.'

Fin flinched. 'Yeah, I know, I saw it on TV.' Fin crossed her arms against her chest.

'Bit of a coincidence, two deaths in Callan Park within a week of each other, don't you think? Did Robbie know this Patrick Hill?'

'Got no idea.'

'What about you…did you know him?'

'No, why should I?' She shrugged. 'What's wrong with you anyway?' Fin said. 'You look like shit.'

Jill ignored Fin, resisted the comeback: *Like you can talk.* 'What about Adam Lee, Benjamin Cheung, David Cheung? Ever heard those names?'

'No.'

'Stop playing games with me, Fin. You're lying. You know very well Patrick Hill was your uncle. According to Mrs Hardcastle, Gracie's next-door neighbour, he lived with you from the time your parents died until you were fourteen years old.'

Fin fidgeted. 'Alright then, yeah, but he's not my uncle, he's my half-uncle.'

'It's highly likely Robbie's and Patrick's deaths are related. Same location, plus blood relatives. If you know anything, anything at all Fin, you need to tell me and tell me now. It could help us find out what really happened to Robbie.'

'Sometimes, bad things happen for a reason.' Fin lit another cigarette, took a drag and blew the smoke into the air. 'Anyway, Robbie committed suicide, didn't he?' Fin looked at Jill. 'Why are you looking at me like that?'

'Like what?' Jill asked.

'Like I'm fuckin' crazy or something.' Fin stood up and grabbed onto the edge of the kitchen counter. 'Think it's time you left.'

# FORTY

RIMIS WAS AT HIS DESK, feet up. There was a knock at the door. He jerked forward, opened his eyes and dropped his feet to the floor. Today Choi was wearing an orange jumper, teamed with a knitted black-and-white striped beret. Rimis thought she was doing a good impression of a teapot cosy.

'Don't just stand there, Choi, come in and sit down.' Rimis sat upright and straightened his tie; embarrassed he'd been caught napping. 'So, what is it?'

She stood at the door. 'Have you forgotten the meeting? Chapman's ordered pizzas.'

He had forgotten. He got to his feet and walked with Choi down the hall to the major incident room. Three boxed pizzas were sitting in the middle of the table, a pile of white paper napkins and bottles of water next to them. The room was humid and the smell of pepperoni overpowering.

The team was assembled when Rimis arrived. Rawlings was standing by the window with a slice of pizza in his hand, while Brennan and Chapman were sitting at the meeting table with notepads in front of them. When Rimis sat down, everyone stopped talking. Rawlings took his assigned seat. Choi sat down next to Rimis and offered him pizza but he waved his hand. She closed the pizza box and pushed it away.

Rimis cleared his throat. 'Welcome back, Brennan. Hope you enjoyed your holiday.' A few light-hearted sniggers broke out around the room. 'Okay, everyone, listen up. As you know, yesterday Brennan discovered Patrick Hill was actually Robbie and Fin's uncle, at least half-uncle.' He motioned to Brennan and she gave a nod. Rimis continued. 'He changed his name by deed poll from Patrick Reilly to Patrick Hill. We have unconfirmed claims he sexually assaulted Fin Calloway when she was a minor and he was behind the wheel when Mr and Mrs Calloway died in a fatal car accident. Chapman, you've been looking into the grandmother's will.'

'Yes, boss.' Calloway tugged at his tie. 'Robbie and Fin Calloway were the only beneficiaries, which means she'd cut her son, Patrick Hill /Reilly out of her will completely. Hill must have been pissed, maybe even driven to kill.'

'What if Hill hadn't died, he might have had Fin in his sights,' Jill said. 'With Robbie and Fin out of the way, it would have left the way open for him to step up and claim his inheritance.'

'But surely Hill could have contested the will through the courts, without resorting to murder,' Choi said. 'And he hardly needed the money, he had enough didn't he?'

'For some people there's no such thing as enough.' Rimis looked at Choi trying not to focus on her beret. 'Money's right up there when it comes to motive for murder. He may have also regarded the inheritance as his right.'

'But Patrick Hill?' Choi furrowed her brow. 'He was hardly a match for Robbie Calloway. Calloway was one hundred and eighty centimetres and weighed in at ninety-two kilos. And it's unlikely now Hill's dead. That's if we're looking at the same perp for both deaths.'

Rimis gave a quick nod. 'Yes, but that doesn't necessarily mean he wasn't involved in Calloway's death in some way. And two people dead at the same location…they must be linked. Especially given the victims are blood relatives.'

'So if we're treating Robbie's death as suspicious our only suspect is Hill but he's not much use to us now he's dead.' Brennan leaned across and grabbed a slice of pizza.

'Of course it may turn out Robbie and Patrick Hill were killed by the same person,' Rimis said. 'Or in the case of Hill, we could be looking at manslaughter by criminal negligence.'

'Huh?' Rawlings managed through a mouthful of pizza.

'I was at the morgue with Doctor Ross this morning and part of the afternoon. Her findings confirm Patrick Hill died from a heart attack. The shot to the forehead was inflicted post-mortem.'

'Who shoots a guy who's already dead?' Rawlings asked.

'Good, question, Luke but it's not who, but why,' Rimis said. 'We could be looking at someone who wanted him dead or at least to give him a good scare. And if murder was the intention, they may have felt they were cheated out of killing him, so they shot him anyway to satisfy themselves.' Rimis leaned over and grabbed a slice of pizza, which was looking more enticing by the minute. 'Anything from the public?'

Choi shook her head. 'Nothing to get excited about and we don't have any witness statements because there weren't any witnesses to either death.'

Rimis held his tie and took a large bite of pizza.

Brennan ran her eye over her notes. 'Here's what we know about Patrick Hill,' she said. 'He was a man of habit, he liked his routine, so what was he doing at the tower? It wasn't part of his normal route. He only found Calloway because the dog led him into the courtyard where the tower is. I'd have thought the clock tower would be the last place he'd want to be.'

'He could have been meeting someone,' Choi said.

'Yes, but who and why?' Rimis glanced around at his team.

'Or maybe Hill was just in the wrong place at the wrong time,' Chapman said. 'He walks into the courtyard to take another look at the tower, indulges his curiosity, but comes across someone who's there for the same reason. Something happens, robbery gone wrong? His wallet was, is, missing. A druggie? He has a heart attack but the perp shoots him anyway. It makes him feel better.' Chapman formed a gun with his fingers and held it to his head.

'Or what if Calloway's death was a planned murder, an attempt to divert us away from the real target, the second death…Patrick Hill?' Choi asked.

Rimis sighed. Too many theories. 'We need much better profiles of Patrick Hill and Robbie Calloway.' He turned to Choi. 'Choi, you were looking at the latest footage from the CCTV cameras. What did you find?'

'No, luck,' Choi said. 'They're still having teething problems with the installation. They did take Jill's advice and installed extra cameras to cover the tower and the eastern gates, but they were misconfigured. There are no visuals.'

'Shit. What about you, Chapman? Have you started on Hill's computer yet?'

'Yes, boss. I've been going through his emails but nothing to report.'

Rimis nodded and turned to Rawlings. 'Rawlings, you found out Hill had a key to the tower, didn't you?'

'Yeah, he's the secretary of the Friends of Callan Park. They run tours of the asylum a couple of times a year. He's got keys to the Kirkbride tunnels as well. The secretary told me Hill lost his set a few months back and they had another set cut. He had a habit of leaving them in the locks. Look, I've been thinking, boss —'

'That'll be a first.' Choi laughed. Chapman sniggered.

'Quiet,' Rimis said. 'Let's hear what Rawlings has to say.'

'I'm still wondering if it's political. It might have something to do with the Callan Park Trust Plan.'

Choi looked across the table at Rawlings. 'Luke actually has a point. It might be worth checking with the Department of Planning and the Friends of Callan Park to see if they've received any nasty threats or petitions recently.'

'You mentioned that before I went on leave, Luke,' Brennan said. 'Haven't you followed it up yet?'

Luke paused mid-gulp, then said: 'We're not all the obsessive types like you, Brennan.'

Before Jill could get a word in Rimis gave her a warning glare then turned to Rawlings. 'Look into it Rawlings, but don't go stepping on anybody's toes. The last thing we need right now is to get the media whipped up into a frenzy. The official line is that these two deaths are unrelated. At this stage we aren't mentioning the bullet wound to Hill's head. We need to keep that information from the public for the moment. And we're still looking for Calloway's gun. The bullet from Hill has been sent to ballistics and given the ballistic fingerprints of all police guns are in the database we should know soon enough if the bullet was fired by Calloway's gun. If the bullet *was* fired from his gun, the most likely person with access is Fin Calloway.'

Jill nodded. 'I don't know what she's capable of, boss. She's not exactly emotionally stable.'

'No,' Rimis replied. 'And it looks like Robbie Calloway was worried enough about his sister's mental state to be looking into treatment for her. Which explains his laptop's browser history of mental health sites.' Jill had been right all along, but he hadn't trusted her instincts.

The meeting went on for a further fifteen minutes. The time was spent going over what they knew, point by point. There was a chain of events beginning with Calloway's death. Rimis brought up the white feathers. 'Brennan has a theory about the feathers we found up in the tower and in Hill's mouth. Brennan?'

'You've probably heard about the practice of young women handing out white feathers to men out of uniform during WW1, to imply that the man was a coward. But during my research I found they have another meaning. Some people believe that guardian angels and dead loved ones send white feathers to comfort their charges. The feathers mean your guardian angel is close, that you're being protected.'

Choi crossed her arms. 'But how does that relate to Robbie and Hill?'

Jill shrugged. 'I don't know…yet.'

After a few moments of silence, Rimis stood up. 'Okay people, we've got lots of theories to chase down. We need to find out who or why someone wanted Robbie Calloway and Patrick Hill dead. We'll start with Hill's detailed life history and I want twenty-four-hour surveillance of the clock tower, and that goes for Patrick Hill's house, as well.' Rimis turned back to the interactive smart board and looked at the photos of Robbie Calloway and Patrick Hill. Alongside them he drew an arrow and scribbled down Fin Calloway's name and followed it by adding a question mark.

'I think it's time we called Fin Calloway in for a friendly chat,' Rimis said. 'Choi why don't you speak to her, given Brennan knows Fin personally. And Brennan you seem to have made an impression on Adam Lee. I want you to pay him a visit, see if there's a connection between him, the Calloways or Hill.'

# FORTY-ONE

ADAM LEE TURNED ON THE television set in the airless room off the kitchen of his father's Chinese restaurant. Along with the television set, the room contained an old sofa, a single bed, drums of cooking oil, sacks of rice and a bar fridge.

Adam grabbed a beer from the fridge and slumped down on the sofa. The television was switched on and a news update droned in the background. Adam looked up when he caught something about a passenger jet crashing in Eastern Ukraine. An act of terror, the news presenter said. A break for an ad and then…

'Patrick… Patrick Hill.'

Adam turned the volume up and watched while the news camera panned Callan Park, then the camera moved in for a close-up shot of the clock tower. A woman reporter was talking about the body that had been discovered earlier that morning — Patrick Hill, a sixty-eight-year-old man who lived in Glover Street across from the Park. He was described as a retired businessman and the person whose dog had discovered a police officer's body at Callan Park a week ago.

A photo of Patrick Hill flashed onto the screen, followed by Robbie Calloway in his police dress uniform. Mention was made of the deaths happening in the same location. They said nothing about Patrick being shot, only that he had died from a heart attack. Adam wondered what the police were playing at. All he could think of was what he knew from the police crime shows he watched on television, the investigators often held back information to eliminate crank suspects from admitting to a crime they hadn't committed.

Adam was relying on Fin to incriminate herself. Her drinking was out of control and he knew she'd been having blackouts. She certainly had a motive to kill Hill. If it came out Hill had abused Fin when she was a child, the police would be looking at her, for sure.

Adam tried to remember if there was anything he'd overlooked but he was confident there was no evidence to link him to the deaths of either Robbie or Patrick, apart from Robbie's gun. He put his magazine down and thought about the Gweilo female detective who'd come to see him in the hospital after the attack at the Interchange. This was the worst part; wondering if she was smart enough to work it out. When Fin had told him the detective and her brother had been friends, it had been the first piece of bad luck — he hoped his luck would hold out.

There was a loud knock on the back door.

Adam swung the door open. Fin was on the doorstep.

'Oh, it's you. What do you want?' Adam stepped back into the room and Fin walked past him. 'Geez,' he said, 'you look like the walking dead.'

Fin clasped her hands. 'It's Uncle Patrick. He's dead, it's all over the news.'

'Of course, he's fucking dead. You killed him, remember?' Adam whispered.

'I did?' Fin looked at Adam and trembled.

'I was there with you. You had Robbie's gun. I had to take it off you. Don't you remember?'

Fin paced the room. 'What's going on? Have you been lacing my stuff with something, some sort of mind-altering shit?'

192

'Keep your voice down, will you? Someone will hear you. Anyway, the way you've been acting it's got nothing to do with me.' Adam stepped back and held up his hands in protest. 'Promise on my dead mum's grave.'

Fin bit into her lip. 'Where's Robbie's gun? We have to get rid of it.'

Adam bent down on his knees and pulled it out from behind a loose brick in the wall. It was wrapped in plastic. He passed it to her.

She stared at it but didn't take it. 'Get rid of it,' she said.

'I wiped it clean. Thought I'd keep it as a souvenir.'

'No. It's Robbie's gun. I don't want you using it.' Fin looked away.

'How did you get it anyway? Didn't think cops took their guns home with them.'

'Robbie was going to threaten Uncle Patrick with it. Robbie always told me he'd get Uncle Patrick one day. He wanted him behind bars for everything he'd done to us. He must have wanted to scare Uncle Patrick into a confession. It was only my word against his with Gracie dead.' She stared at the gun again. 'I can't remember being with Uncle Patrick at the tower but I remember taking the stairs to the top. My memory's a blank.' Fin frowned. 'Oh, Adam, what are we going to do?'

He shrugged, took a swig of beer. 'I don't know what you're going to do, but there's no way I'm going down for murder. Here, take the gun.'

Fin knocked Adam's can of beer to the floor as she rushed from the room.

# FORTY-TWO

Jɪʟʟ ᴄʀᴏssᴇᴅ Vɪᴄᴛᴏʀɪᴀ Aᴠᴇɴᴜᴇ ᴀᴛ the traffic lights and walked into the Old Shanghai restaurant. Adam's father, Guang Lee, owned the restaurant. Jill figured if she had to speak to Adam Lee she might as well order some food from the take-away menu.

'Can I order braised chicken with cashews to take-away?'

Jill looked at the gold money cat next to the cash register. The cat's left paw was raised. Jenny Choi had told her the right paw invites money and good fortune while the left invites customers. Judging by the number of people in the restaurant tonight, the cat wasn't doing its job.

The woman handed Jill her change and passed the order through the open servery to the chef.

'Is Adam about?' Jill flashed her ID at the woman behind the counter.

Jill saw the concerned look on the woman's face. 'I don't want trouble.

He's out the back.' She jerked her chin to the left. 'Through the kitchen, first door on right.'

The soles of Jill's shoes stuck to the floor when she walked into the tiny kitchen. Jill nodded at the chef and stopped to watch as he ladled sauce into a large wok. He gave her a sideward glance and, as if on cue, the wok sizzled and burst into flame. Aniseed, cinnamon, garlic. The aromatic spices reminded Jill of how hungry she was.

At the end of a narrow passage Jill walked past a fire exit and turned to the right. The door looked brand new. And cheap, maybe a Bunning's stock item. Jill knocked and wondered what sort of reception she would get from Adam Lee now that he was on his home turf.

No answer. Jill waited, knocked again.

'Piss off, Fin. I don't want to talk to you,' came Adam Lee's voice through the door.

'It's Detective Brennan from Chatswood Police.' Jill turned the door handle and stepped into the room. She stopped dead in her tracks. She hadn't expected Adam to be on all fours wiping the floor with his t-shirt. His upper torso, bare, a very interesting tattoo on display.

Adam looked up at her. 'It's you? I thought it was someone else,' Adam said. 'What are you doing here?' Adam got to his feet and grabbed a t-shirt from the grubby sofa. He turned his back on Jill and struggled to get the t-shirt over his head.

Jill hoped the surprise wouldn't show in her voice. 'I was hungry, thought I'd order some Chinese take-away. Knew you lived here so...what were you doing just know? It smells like a brewery in here.'

'Had an accident, spilt me beer, didn't I.'

Adam grabbed another can of beer from the bar fridge. He pointed the can in her direction. 'Want one?' He popped the top.

Jill shook her head. 'How's the chest?'

'Still hurts but it's better than it was.'

'Miss? Your order is ready.'

Jill turned around. The woman who had taken her order handed Jill a bag with her take-away inside.

'I added prawn chips, no charge for you.'

Jill was shaken but hoped it didn't show. She took the bag from the woman and thanked her. She turned back to Adam. 'I'd better go. Glad to see you're looking so well, Adam.' She took a step towards the door, stopped, and turned around. 'You thought I was Fin just now. Fin's an unusual name.' Jill grabbed the door handle.

Adam ignored the comment, instead saying, 'Enjoy your take-away.'


Jill walked in through the front doors of Chatswood Police Station.

'What are you doing here? You're not rostered on tonight.' The station officer leant over the counter. 'But I see you've brought me my dinner. Smells, good.'

'Yeah, in your dreams.' Jill looked towards the stairs. 'Listen, something's come up; I have to talk to the boss. Is he in his office?'

'No and you won't find anybody else upstairs either. We're operating on a skeleton staff. Everyone's been called out to a house in Mowbray Road. There's been a brawl between two teenage gangs. Five teenagers were taken to North Shore Hospital.'

Jill hesitated, mulling over whether to log in from home to submit the report on Adam Lee or go up to her desk. In the end the food was the decider. Better to eat it hot at her desk than re-heat it at home. 'I need to log a report. And I'll eat my take-away while I'm at it.' Jill held the plastic bag up for the station officer to smell.

The station officer shook his head.

Jill walked up the stairs to the detectives' room. She sat down at her desk and opened the plastic bag, crunched on a prawn chip and pulled out a fork and the container of food. She took a mouthful of chicken and logged onto her computer. Her visit to the restaurant had been a lucky break. She'd been surprised to see the tattoo, the circle with the red Chinese characters on Adam Lee's stomach. So, Adam Lee was a member of the Red Cave Gang. He hadn't meant for her to see it. She knew what it meant and Adam Lee knew, she knew. And Fin? Adam Lee must be the boy Katrina Andrel had told her Robbie was worried about hanging around Fin. She thought about phoning Rimis to share her discovery with him but decided it could wait until tomorrow. He would have plenty on his plate at the moment. And besides she was wrecked. If she had an early night she'd be in a better position in the morning to face whatever the day threw at her.

She dumped the empty container in the bin and logged a report on Adam Lee. Fifteen minutes later, she shut down the computer and grabbed her shoulder bag. She pulled on her coat and prepared herself for the cold shock of the street after the warmth of the station. On her way out she said goodnight to the station officer.

When Jill arrived back at her car, light rain was falling. Would the rain ever stop? She started the car and headed home. The road sparkled with the glare of headlights, cars whooshed by and all she could think about was getting home.

Jill parked her car, locked it and ran through a line of puddles to the front door of her apartment block. The body corporate still hadn't organised the security system they'd promised. She made a mental note to call her landlord tomorrow and talk to him about it.

Jill ran her hand through her damp hair and pressed the automatic light sensor before she climbed the stairs to her apartment. All was quiet in the stairwell with no television sets blaring or lights under the doors of her neighbours' apartments. The timed lights in the stairwell went out. She didn't bother to switch them on again. When she reached the second floor, she froze.

No…how could it be?

The door to her apartment was ajar. She pulled out her gun, released the safety, held it out in front of her and pushed the door open with the tip of her boot. She identified herself, scanned the room in front of her and crept around the apartment checking each room as she went. When she walked into her bedroom, she drew a breath. 'Police! Freeze.'

Someone hit her from behind, grabbed her in a headlock. She twisted, tried to break free from the strong grip. The last thing Jill remembered was her attacker's breath. It smelt of aniseed, cinnamon and garlic.

# FORTY-THREE

THE WIND RATTLED THE WINDOWS. Fin had driven straight home after she'd left Adam at the restaurant. She'd had a couple of drinks to calm her nerves and then stumbled into bed. But her mind couldn't let go. Her hands shook even though she was lying down, and every now and again her breathing became so fast she thought she might pass out. Had she really shot Patrick with Robbie's gun, like Adam said? And what about Robbie? Had he taken his own life or had something else happened the night he died? Something so terrifying that Fin didn't even want to think about it. But she knew the answer to her questions lay in the dream, the same dream she'd dreamt every night since Robbie had died, but it was beyond her reach. After tossing and turning all night she closed her eyes and at last sleep came to her.

The soft rain fell on her face. She tipped her head back and opened her mouth. She swayed and giggled, rattled the high gates and smiled when she found them open. She ran towards the courtyard. There was something comforting about the confined space of the tower, even though the walls were damp and the smell of mould made her sneeze. She looked through the open arches to the far side of the river. She thought of Robbie and knew he'd come; he'd promised her. And Robbie always kept his promises.

'Fin, for God's sake!'

She heard Robbie's voice and looked down.

'What are you doing up there? Come down here, now! I'm getting soaked.'

Fin could only just hear him through the beating rain.

After a few moments he repeated: 'I said, come down.'

Fin moved away from the edge. When she reached the bottom she pushed against the tower's timber door and ran to him. He was standing in the thudding rain with his arms crossed against his chest, his head bowed.

When she ran to him, he grabbed her by the shoulders and shook her. 'What are you doing for Christ's sake?'

Fin grabbed his hand and they ran for shelter inside the tower. Robbie brushed himself down.

'Robbie? Remember the Jacaranda tree in Gracie's back yard and how we used to hide there from Uncle Patrick? He could never get us up there, could he?' Fin began to sing a song about princesses.

'For Christ's sake, Fin, cut it out.' Robbie pulled the hood of his rain jacket back. 'I'm not in the mood for this shit.' He looked at her. 'And you've been drinking again, you smell like a brewery. And stop making so much noise, there's gotta be a security guy about the place, even in this weather.'

'He's gone off on his rounds; he'll be over by Broughton Hall by now. I know his routine, he never comes into the courtyard.'

'Why did you want to meet here, of all places?' Robbie asked.

'I wanted to show you the view from the tower.'

'Are you crazy, Fin? We're not kids anymore, you have to let go of all that shit.'

He shoved his hands into his pockets. 'I have, you should too. And you're not well. You need medical help.'

She gave a childish grin.

Robbie shook his head. 'How did you get in here, anyway?'

'I've got a key.'

'A key? Where did you get a key?'

'I found it.'

Robbie fingered the lock with his gloved hand.

'Come on,' Fin said, 'don't be such a stick in the mud. This'll be fun.'

'Fin, I'm a police officer, if I'm caught…'

Fin tripped on the first step. 'Are you coming up or not?' She looked over her shoulder and saw the look on her brother's face before she scrambled up the stairs. 'Come on, scaredy cat.' She giggled.

'This is madness.' Robbie shone his torch up the staircase. When he finally reached the top, he was trembling from the cold. His rain jacket was soaked inside and out. He took if off and shook it.

Fin had her back turned to Robbie. She was standing by the open arches, looking at the view. Robbie wiped a drop of rain from his nose.

The rain had stopped. A strong breeze had sprung up and blown open a gap in the clouds to reveal the moon. When he put his hand on Fin's shoulder, she pushed him away. She flung her arms wide and threw her head back.

'Welcome to my castle.' She hiccupped.' Look at the view, Robbie. You can't see them now, but the Blue Mountains are over there and the river winds all the way to Parramatta.' She staggered back from the ledge and fell to the stone floor.

Robbie stuffed his rain jacket into his backpack. He found a dry patch on the floor and sat down beside her. He crossed his legs and Fin put her head on his shoulder.

'Can't believe you found Uncle Patrick, after all this time.' Fin's voice was suddenly quiet, child-like.

Robbie had tried to protect her, but what could a small boy do against a grown man, especially a bully and alcoholic? Who was he kidding? He should have done something, tried to protect her. There was no escaping it: he had failed. Failed his little sister.

Fin looked at Robbie. 'What are we going to do about him, now we've found him?'

'I'm going to give him a thrashing,' Robbie said.

'I don't know how Gracie kept Uncle Patrick's secrets for so long.'

'He was her son. Mothers will do anything to protect their children.'

'Maybe,' Fin said. 'But we were her grandchildren.'

'It's not the same, Fin. And anyway, how can you explain or understand the reasons behind what people do.'

'Uncle Patrick should pay for what he did.'

'Don't worry, he's going to pay alright; he's going to pay big time.' Robbie tilted her chin towards him. 'What's wrong? You're crying.'

'I've turned out just like Mad Annie haven't I?'

'What do you mean?'

'I'm crazy. They say it runs in families.' Fin sniffed, wiped her nose with the back of her hand and reached into her backpack. 'I bought my angel feathers with me, I still have a few left.' Fin opened the tin and picked out three feathers.

'I can't believe you've still got them, after all this time.' Robbie smiled. 'I remember Gracie called them your angel calling cards. They were meant to protect you.'

'Here, Robbie.' Fin handed them to him but the feathers fell from his hand.

He looked at her. 'It was a big mistake coming here, Fin.'

# FORTY-FOUR

Detective Luke Rawlings knocked on Rimis's door. 'DCI Carver's just arrived, boss. He's downstairs.'

'Good, bring him up to the meeting room.'

Rawlings turned to leave.

'Oh, and ask him if he wants a coffee, will you?'

Ten minutes later, Chief Inspector Carver had the attention of a room full of detectives and uniforms. Rimis surveyed the room, noticed Brennan was missing. What was she up to now?

Carver stood at the front of the room. 'I know you're all busy and I'll try and keep this as brief as possible. We're all under a lot of stress at the moment with these teenage gangs. After the brawl on Mowbray Road last night I thought it was important I come and speak to you in person.' Carver leaned on the desk. 'We've got kids as young as thirteen being assaulted and robbed. The hooligans responsible are demanding cash, phones anything of value. They're generally picking on people their own age and we've seen in places like Hurstville and Campbelltown a lot more incidences of graffiti and tagging. Reported assaults are also escalating.' Carver scanned the room, making eye contact. 'So far this month in Hurstville alone we've charged three teenage males in relation to offences. A sixteen-year-old Hurstville boy has been charged with armed robbery and attempted extortion, and a fourteen-year-old Campbelltown boy has also been charged with criminal damage and drug-related offences.'

He tugged his ear. 'I want to assure you, we are methodically working through the problem and I'm confident we'll be able to stop this anti-social behaviour from escalating further.' He turned to Jenny Choi. 'Choi. You're the community liaison officer; I want you to reassure the community. I want the message to get out there that if they're approached, we don't want people to put themselves in a situation where they're at risk. People have the right to go about their business without being intimidated.'

Choi gave a nod.

'Now, are there any questions?' Carver said.

'Sir?'

'Yes?' Carver turned to Luke. 'It's Rawlings, isn't it?'

'Yes, sir. Do you think Vincent Wan is behind these gangs? And if he is, are we any closer to tracking him down?'

'Good question, Rawlings. There are many reasons why these gangs are on the rise. Social, cultural reasons and economic reasons are a big part of it, but our Intel suggests Vincent Wan could be directly involved in the gang culture here in Chatswood, but we don't have any solid evidence...yet. But we are getting close. Anymore questions?' Carver looked around the room.

Everyone shook their heads and Rimis led Carver out of the meeting room and down the corridor.

'Got time for a quick lunch?' Rimis asked.

'Thanks, Nick but I've got another meeting at Hurstville. By the way, how's Jill? Shouldn't she have been in that briefing?'

'Actually, I'm not sure where she is.' Rimis looked at his watch. 'It's not like her to miss a meeting.'

'Maybe you should give her a call.'

Rimis gave a half-grunt but didn't bother mentioning he'd already tried her mobile twice. He wanted Carver to think Rimis had some control over his staff. The two men shook hands and said goodbye.

Rimis watched Carver weave his way through the open-plan offices and wondered why Carver appeared so concerned about Brennan. He shrugged, and walked downstairs to the front desk.

'You seen Brennan this morning?' Rimis asked.

'No, but she was in last night,' the station officer said. 'It was just after we got the call about the brawl in Mowbray Road. She asked if you were in, but you and Detective Choi had just left.'

'Did she say what she wanted to speak to me about?'

He shook his head. 'Nope, but she looked disappointed when I told her you weren't here.'

Rimis walked upstairs to his office. He sat down behind his desk and rang Brennan's mobile phone for the third time. It went to voicemail. Five minutes later he tried again and there was still no answer.

Rimis walked into the detectives' room. 'Anybody seen or heard from Brennan? Choi, you spoken to her?'

'No, boss,' Choi replied while the others shook their heads.

'Well, let me know if she calls.'

Rimis went back into his office and closed the door. All the team knew Carver was coming to the station this morning for a meeting. It was unlike Jill not to phone in if she was going to miss a station meeting. If he hadn't heard from her by lunch time, he'd send a patrol car over to her apartment.

An hour later Jenny Choi tapped on Rimis's office door and walked in. She pulled up a chair across the table from Rimis and sat down.

'Boss, still no luck with Fin Calloway. I've just come back from her apartment. She wasn't at home and none of the neighbours were either, so I couldn't ask anyone if they'd seen her.'

He leaned forward. 'Get a surveillance team over there. I want her found. She's the only suspect we have, not to mention the only surviving member of the Calloway family. She could even be the next victim. I want two shifts in six-hour rotations. The moment she turns up, I want to know about it. And make sure they have a good description of her.'

'She shouldn't be too hard to spot if she's in the neighbourhood,' Choi said. 'There aren't many Caucasian, six-feet-tall women walking around Chatswood.'

'Mmm…true.' He paused. 'You haven't heard from Jill have you?'

'No. I've phoned her a few times, even sent her a couple of texts to tell her we wanted to speak to her.'

For the past few hours Rimis had been trying to convince himself Brennan was off doing her own thing, as usual. That she'd walk into the office any minute and he'd tell her off for missing the meeting and not reporting in that day. But now? It had been too long. 'Something's not right.' Rimis pushed his chair back and stood up. 'I want you to organise a patrol car to go to Brennan's place. And let me know immediately if you hear from either Brennan or Fin Calloway.'

'Yes, boss.'

Choi left and Rimis tried to stay still, tried not to pace. The next half an hour dragged by, but finally his landline rang — Jenny Choi.

'Well?' Rimis ran his hand through his hair.

'The patrol car just called in…Jill's front door wasn't locked and there were signs of a struggle inside the apartment. It was a right mess.'

'Shit!' Rimis hung up, walked down the corridor to the detectives' room.

Choi was still holding the phone, her face ashen.

Rimis took a deep breath. 'Listen up, everyone. Brennan's missing.' All eyes were on him. 'As far as I know, the duty officer was the last person to see her, at around eight o'clock last night. Rawlings, see if we can get a trace on Jill's mobile phone. And Chapman, I want you to check if she logged onto the police network last night.'

'Right, boss,' Choi said.

Rimis remembered Fin. 'Choi any word on Fin Calloway yet?'

'No, boss.'

'Great, just great. So she's missing as well?'

When Rimis walked back into his office, his mobile phone rang. It was Scott Carver.

'Have you heard from Jill?' Scott asked.

'No. And I just got word from a patrol car I sent over there…signs of a struggle at her apartment. They checked with one of the neighbours but he said he didn't hear or see anything. He was out, didn't get home until well past midnight. I'm worried, Scotty. Really worried. With all this digging around she's been doing, maybe she's upset someone.' Rimis leaned over the phone and rubbed his forehead. 'The wrong someone.'

Chapman knocked on the door and Rimis waved him into his office. 'Hang on will you?' He looked up at Chapman. 'What is it, Chapman? Did you find something?'

'Jill logged a report last night. She went to see Adam Lee at his father's restaurant. She saw a tattoo on his stomach that identified him as a member of the Red Cave Gang.'

Rimis's shoulders slumped. 'Shit.' Rimis brought the mouthpiece closer. 'Did you hear that?'

'I heard,' Scott Carver said.

# FORTY-FIVE

JILL WANTED TO SCREAM FROM the blinding pain behind her eyes but her mouth was stuffed with an oily rag and covered in tape. The rag was small, no bigger than the palm of her hand she guessed, but if it worked its way any further down her throat she'd choke. Her wrists were bound together in front of her. A blindfold dug into her temples — tied tight. Her head pounded, sinuses screaming in pain. Her first response was to check her holster but it was empty. The Swiss army knife she always carried with her and her phone were missing as well. Her gun. What use had it been to her? She'd been given special permission to take the Glock home because she feared for her safety. Dorin Chisca had threatened her life when she'd gone to speak to him in prison about the part he played in her father's murder. Chisca was a powerful man, with many friends inside and outside of prison.

Every nerve in her body was on high alert. All she could remember was being grabbed from behind and then it all went hazy. Think harder. Jill's breathing slowed. She remembered the shadow by the window, the attack from behind, and the biting sting of a needle. She went through everything she could remember; looking for any detail that might help her identify her attackers.

*Brennan, you fool.* She'd identified Adam Lee as a member of the Red Cave Gang, hadn't she? What the hell did she think was going to happen?

She had to regain her composure. Where was she? She felt around her with her fingers. The space was small, she tried to kick her legs out but they thudded against surfaces in every direction. Car boot? Seemed likely, but the car was stationary…it was parked somewhere. How long had she been unconscious?

Try to breathe, stay calm. At least she wasn't going to run out of air. Cars weren't built tight enough for that…were they? And the lock? They're meant to be secure from the outside in, not the other way around, right? A release tag, there should be one, somewhere.

Then she felt it. Not a release tag. It crawled across her cheek, spiky appendages pricked at her skin. Movement in her hair. She was living her worst nightmare. She shook her head from side to side, tried to raise her bound hands to her face, tried to flick the cockroach away. Get the fuck off. Tears flowed.

She kicked out. Then the rag edged slightly backwards in her mouth. She could feel its hot sting — close to the point where her gag reflex would kick in. She froze. Calm down, Jill. Get it together.

She focused on taking more even breaths through her nose. Slow, solid, but not too deep. Her heart rate slowed. Okay. She had to get out. Run. But where to? She had no idea where she was. She concentrated, listened for any sound that would help identify her location. She heard a plane overhead, a barking dog, distant traffic noise. She rolled back and forth trying to loosen her bindings. The car rocked and rolled with her. She bent her wrists, bent them further until she thought they would break.

Over and over she repeated the action until her wrists were raw. Her sense of time was distorted, but at a guess she'd been working the ropes for at least half an hour, maybe an hour. Her hands cramped. She lay still, listened to her laboured breathing, thought of Rimis. Would he come charging to her rescue like he had when Kevin Taggart had tried to kill her? How long had she been in the boot? She might have only been unconscious for a few hours. If that was the case, it was still the middle of the night. No one would realise she was missing. And by the time they did it might be too late. No, it was up to her, she couldn't wait for a non-existent cavalry to turn up and save her. She tried the ropes again, tugging, twisting her wrists, and working the rope, again and again until she felt them loosen a little. With her energy spent, she knew she was dehydrated and the ache behind her eyes made her wonder what damage had been done to her skull.

She rested, gathered her strength, and began all over again. Had it been two hours now? Three? She twisted her shoulders from side to side, struggled with the rope until it was loose enough for her to feel the circulation returning to her torso and hands. Whoever she was dealing with, they weren't professionals. She'd just had her first lucky break. Second lucky break: whoever tied these knots had never been a boy scout. And they'd tied her wrists in front of her, not behind her back.

The rope was loose enough now that she could lean over and tear the masking tape from her mouth with her fingers. The rush of heat and pain seared her lips and cheeks. She yanked the foul-tasting rag from her mouth, felt saliva and bile dribble down her chin. Next, she tugged her blindfold, pulled it down and blinked. Cars had tool kits, right? She groped with her fingers, used them to lift up the worn, carpeted panel to the tyre well. She backed herself into the corner of the boot and for once she was glad of her height — or lack thereof.

She reached into the tyre well. A lone screwdriver. It would have to do. She used the tool to loosen the knots further. She rolled over onto her side, and felt for a boot release. Nothing. The car must be an old model, pre-2000. She felt for the lock with her fingers, found it and jabbed the point of the screwdriver against it to try and release the spring latch. She pressed her back hard into the corner of the boot and kicked her feet out with every ounce of energy she had left.

The boot sprung open enough for her to push it up with her legs. She climbed over the rim, projected herself out and fell hands-first onto a slab of concrete. She lay there to catch her breath. She tasted blood, tried to stand. Fell. Pin pricks of white light flashed and exploded in her head.

# FORTY-SIX

BLOOD POUNDED JILL'S EARS. She got to her feet, touched the back of her head, felt the open wound with her fingers: wet and sticky from blood.

The scent of exotic spices was powerful. She recognised the car that had held her captive— a 1999 Commodore VL. Her father had had one just like it.

After she'd pushed the boot closed, a thought struck her. What if her abductors weren't coming back? It was obvious she was dealing with amateurs. Maybe they didn't have the guts to kill her. It was possible they'd decided to take the easy way out and let her die in the boot.

She looked around. Searched for a way out. Saw an illuminated exit sign. She was in large industrial warehouse, the only windows, at ceiling height, were blacked out.

She was sweating from struggling in the boot, but now the cold hit her and she started shaking. She knew she had to move, get out of here in case they were coming back for her.

Why had she been brought, here? If they'd wanted her dead why not kill her in her apartment? And how did they get into her apartment, anyway? With so many locks it was like Fort Knox. She didn't want to think about anything now except getting out of the warehouse. One thing she did know, if she got out of this alive she was packing up her things and handing back the keys to her apartment. She would never feel safe there again, not after this.

But for now, she had to work out who she was dealing with. Adam Lee wasn't smart enough to have organised her abduction on his own. So who was he in league with? Vincent Wan?

Then a low growl of a metal roller door. A wedge of low light. The door didn't go all the way up. Footsteps on concrete. Jill looked around for a place to hide. She crouched behind a pallet of boxes in a dark corner, shivering uncontrollably.

'It was a mistake bringing her here. I want you to kill her, and then leave the country. Think you can manage that, Shazi?'

'Do I have to do it now? I was hoping to have fun with her first.'

Jill knew that voice. It was Adam Lee.

'No time for that.'

The other man's voice had an edge to it. He wasn't used to having his instructions questioned.

'We have drawn too much attention to ourselves already. Now get that roller door down before someone sees us. And turn the lights on.' The door hit the ground with a loud ker-clunk. Industrial lights lit up the warehouse like a Jersey Jack pinball machine.

A car door opened, then the boot. Slam. Mumbled voices.

'Where are you, Detective Brennan?' came the mocking voice of Adam Lee.

She crawled in behind another wooden pallet stacked high with sacks of rice. Moments later, she heard heavy breathing, the stink of garlic and cooking oil. Never show weakness, never show fear, Rimis's words cycled over and over in her head.

She held her breath, waiting. With no way of escaping, Jill knew it wouldn't be long before they found her. She patted the pocket of her jeans, her only hope. They were getting closer now, kicking empty boxes, and rattling steel shelving.

A figure stepped towards her; his face hidden by shadow.

'Shame you saw my tattoo.' Adam was breathing hard, and despite the cold Jill could smell the fetid stench of sweat and rage. Adam grabbed her by both arms and dragged her out from her hiding place.

Jill kicked him. She looked at the older man and recognised him from photos she'd seen — Vincent Wan. She looked him directly in the eye. 'Are you aware of the mandatory sentencing laws in this country for killing police officers? It's life imprisonment if you don't know?'

'You really think I'm interested in your Australian laws?' Vincent Wan said.

Jill tried to pull away again but Adam held her tight. Wan traced the line of her cheekbone, pushing a strand of hair behind her ear.

Jill stopped struggling. 'You're making it worse for yourself, Mr Wan.' She said his name with purpose.

'Very good, Detective. I am honoured you recognise me.' Wan came closer looked her in the eye. 'You can tell a lot from a person's eyes. Don't you think?'

Jill squinted, ignored his question.

Wan pulled a gun from the waistband of his trousers. 'You've met my nephew, haven't you? I call him Shazi. A nickname I have for him. It means idiot in Mandarin. Unfortunately, he takes after my brother in the intelligence department. I give him a simple instruction: abduct Benjamin Cheung, but what does he do? He allows the boy to overpower him. I realise now it is

true what they say; if you want something done proper-
ly, you must do it yourself.'

Adam's grip tightened.

'Why didn't Benjamin Cheung come forward?' Jill
asked Wan.

'Because, my dear, he and his family knew who
they were dealing with.'

'So you extorted money from the family and went
ahead and killed David Cheung anyway.'

'Yes, but never mind that, unfortunately, the
mother and son are out of my reach for now, but not
for long.'

'What about Lucy Fletcher the girl who was run
down the same night David Cheung was murdered?'

'Yes, very unfortunate. Another one of Shazi's
careless mistakes. She was being held here, but she
managed to escape. Her death was an accident. The girl
was not meant to die, my men were careless. She was
dressed in dark clothes they simply didn't see her run
out in front of them. Such a waste. She was a beautiful
girl and would have brought in a tidy sum when I...'

'You bastard.' Jill clenched her knuckles so hard
they ached.

Wan glared at Adam. 'Get some rope. And make
sure you do a better job of it this time. We'll dispose of
her at another location.'

Adam stomped off.

'You won't get away with this.' Jill pushed her chin
out, forced a steely edge into her voice even though it
was an act. Was her life really going to end like this?

'That's where you are wrong, Detective. I am a
powerful man. I have influence over many people.'

What a mess. She was in way over her head this
time and sensed this would be her only chance. When

217

she heard Adam pop the boot she felt for the screwdriver in her pocket.

Wan turned his head. 'What are you doing, Shazi? Hurry up. The detective and I have finished our conversation.' He turned back to Jill and stepped closer. A barrel of a gun, solid, metallic in his hand was aimed at her chest. 'I'm becoming impatient and when I am impatient, I am dangerous.'

Jill's fingers closed around the handle of the screwdriver in her pocket. He was close enough. It was now or never. She struck out at him but misjudged the blow. The gun fell to the ground. A single shot fired into the air. Jill tripped, straightened up and tried to run for the roller doors. Wan grabbed her from behind, spun her around, retaliated by slamming his fist in her face. Jill's head snapped back, blood running from her nose. Her breath was jagged. Have to find the gun. Her head spinning from the blow, pounding, pounding. Her vision blurred. Banging on the metal roller door. Voices shouting, heavy footsteps, running, getting closer, no time. Wan's back up.

Jill got to her feet. The gun. Heard the click of the safety, tried to forget the memory of bodies ripped open by bullets. She didn't move, didn't blink. She was about to die. She heard a sharp crack. Jill toppled forward and felt the thud of concrete against her forehead.

# FORTY-SEVEN

THE STENCH OF ANTISEPTIC AND the clatter of metal and trolley wheels rolling along the linoleum corridors had woken her. Jill didn't open her eyes. It was a miracle she'd escaped with only a couple of broken ribs, concussion, an array of cuts and grazes and four stitches to the back of her head. Thankfully, her nose wasn't broken.

From the time she was allowed visitors Bea and Harry had visited and now it was Rimis's turn. Jill was confused about what had happened in the warehouse — how they'd found her, how she'd got out. And who'd fired the shot? Had they got Wan?

'You gave us the real run-around this time, Brennan. When I saw you on the ground I thought...' Rimis's voice was soft.

'You were there?'

He nodded.

So the cavalry did come. 'Who else?' she asked.

'Choi, Carver and four uniforms,' Rimis said.

Jill nodded and looked over at the flowers and cards on the shelf opposite her bed.

'Vincent Wan and Adam Lee?'

'Wan didn't make it. The bullet nicked his heart. He made it to the hospital, but he died on the table.' Rimis moved closer to the bed and put his hand on her shoulder.

Wan was no saint, but his life had been taken. After a few seconds Jill looked at Rimis. 'Who fired the shot?'

'You won't believe me when I tell you.'

'Try me.' Jill sat up and adjusted her hospital gown.

'Constable Patullo. Rimis's hand fell back to his side. 'He saved your life, Jill.'

Jill took a few moments to take it in. She wiped her eyes with the heels of her hands. 'Looks like I owe him a drink.'

Rimis nodded.

'So, tell me about Adam Lee,' Jill said.

'The scum's in custody. Speaking of Adam Lee, we found your mobile phone in the front seat of Lee's car. I charged it for you.'

Jill gave a small nod and smiled. 'I've been wondering, how did you know where to find me?'

'When Chapman first looked through Robbie's laptop, he found a Google Earth search of an old warehouse. It was the last thing Robbie had been looking at before he died. Chapman printed it out for me but I didn't know what it meant at the time so I filed it without realising its significance. Plus back then we'd...I mean *I* was sure it was suicide.' Rimis edged back toward the end of the bed and sat near Jill's feet. 'And then Rawlings showed me the map you'd highlighted. We were in the middle of checking all the warehouses in the area when we received an unconfirmed sighting of Vincent Wan at Chatswood Mall by an off-duty constable. She thought she recognised him from photos, so she followed him back to Chatswood Chase parking station. A photo of Wan was sent through to her mobile phone and once she confirmed it was Wan, we tailed him to the warehouse.'

'Scott Carver must be very pleased with himself. Another notch in his belt.' Jill sank back into the pillows, suddenly very tired.

'Jill, there's something you should know, you'll find out anyway.' Rimis tugged at his collar and loosened his tie.

'What? More bad news?'

'I'm afraid so. It's about Robbie.'

'Yes.' Jill barely had the energy to listen.

'When we reminded Adam Lee that with Vincent Wan dead he was on his own, he became very co-operative. Apparently Robbie found out Adam was supplying Fin with drugs and suspected Adam had some more sinister associates. Robbie would have heard about the task force Carver was setting up into Asian gangs and, it's only a theory, but I imagine he would have thought Adam could have been connected — drugs and gangs always go together. Or else he was trying to protect Fin, trying to get her away from Adam. Then Adam found out Robbie was investigating him.' Rimis shifted on the bed and crossed his legs awkwardly. 'Adam told us Wan ordered one of his henchmen to make Robbie disappear. He was watching Robbie's house and followed him to Callan Park and the tower when he went to meet Fin the night he died. Apparently Wan's man found Robbie and Fin arguing at the top. Told Wan that Fin was so pissed Santa Claus could have been there and she wouldn't have known. She was on the edge, threatening to jump. Robbie grabbed her and pushed her to safety but before he could climb down himself he lost his balance, slipped and fell. It wasn't suicide, but it wasn't murder either. Just a horrible accident.'

'So Robbie didn't kill himself.' Jill looked at Rimis. 'Robbie would have done anything for Fin, even die for her. Robbie told me once he felt he'd failed Fin. He wouldn't tell me how or why but obviously it was because of Patrick and what he'd done to her. Patrick liked young girls. Jill shuddered, thinking about Fin's horrific life...first her parents were killed, then her uncle abused her and then her brother fell from the clock tower at Callan Park because of her.

Rimis rubbed his chin. 'You were right. Right to fight for Robbie.'

After a few beats, Jill said, 'What about Patrick Hill? He wasn't involved with Wan was he?'

'Actually, he was. But it was through Fin... indirectly.'

Jill frowned.

'Fin told Adam what Hill had done to her, that he like young girls. Adam saw that as a business opportunity. He introduced Patrick to Wan, who was heavily involved in human trafficking and child prostitution.'

'Oh, God.'

'What?'

'When I went to see Hill's neighbour, she mentioned men with children visiting Hill once a month or so. They were...' Jill didn't want to finish the sentence. She followed the law, not vengeance, but either way Patrick Hill and Vincent Wan deserved to be dead. She swallowed back the anger. 'So who shot Hill?'

'Don't know yet for sure. Adam says Fin, but we need her side of the story. Ultimately it will be her word against his. Not that it will matter...the gun shot wound was post-mortem.' He paused. 'But either way Hill was a marked man. According to Adam, Hill tried to get in on Wan's business plan, said he knew plenty of customers who liked kids and wanted a cut, a finder's fee. I don't think Hill realised the sort of people he was dealing with because he actually threatened Wan, said he'd make an anonymous call to the police if he didn't get his way. Adam admitted Wan wanted him to set Fin up for Hill's murder, but then Hill had a heart attack.'

'What about David Cheung?'

'Adam was sent by Wan to kidnap Benjamin Cheung. But Benjamin fought back, got the upper hand and accidentally knifed Adam. At that point Wan stepped in. He threatened David Cheung and his family, told Cheung to pay up or they were all dead.'

'Sounds like Wan was cleaning up his nephew's mess,' Jill said.

Rimis nodded. 'Wan screwed up big time. He'd covered his tracks for years, and then made the mistake of involving Adam Lee in his business. What they say about mixing family and business is true.' Rimis stared out the window, then back at Jill. 'You going to be okay?'

Jill gave a nod. She was glad Robbie didn't kill himself, but maybe this was worse. Robbie was dead because Fin got into bed with the Red Cave Gang. She should have known Robbie would start digging. Fin would have to live with that...if she could make sense of any of it through the booze.

'Any sign of Fin?'

Rimis shook his head.

'Try the Mountains. Maybe she's gone back to Gracie's house.'

# FORTY-EIGHT

FIN WAS NUMB, BUT it wasn't from the cold or from the wind tugging at her jacket. It could be snowing and she wouldn't have noticed. A raindrop landed on her face, made its way gently down her cheek until it reached the point of her chin. Two drops, three, heavier now. Fin leaned a shoulder against a wall of an abandoned building and looked through the trees towards the imposing grey stone of the clock tower - the one place where she felt safe. In some twisted way the tower connected her to her childhood. Was it the story Gracie had told of Mad Annie Calloway, who'd hanged herself from the tower with a makeshift rope made from bed sheets, or was it the forked boughs of the Jacaranda tree in Gracie's backyard that Fin and Robbie climbed to escape Patrick's reach. She supposed there had been a life before Uncle Patrick but she had no memory of it. There were only scraps left, something familiar like a tune in your head that you couldn't get rid of.

Fin reached into the pocket of her rain jacket and pulled out a crumpled passport-sized photograph of Robbie. She studied it, remembered the day it was taken. She and Robbie had gone into the city and stopped at one of those photo kiosks. Robbie's eyes stared back at her like saucers. His mouth was oval-shaped — Robbie playing the clown, doing impressions of the horror movie, *Scream*.

Fin's eyes teared up from the wind. She wiped them with the back of her hand. When had she decided living wasn't worth the effort? Had it been before or after Robbie died?

Rimis reached for his mobile phone on his desk. It was Brennan talking so fast he couldn't even decipher the words.

'Take a breath, Jill. You're not making sense.'

'It's Fin. She phoned me.' Jill's voice was slower, but still edged with panic. 'She's at Callan Park, in the tower. She wants to talk to me, only me; said she'd jump at the first sight of police.'

'Christ, how the hell did she get up there?' Rimis asked.

'Got no idea but I'm on my way there now.'

'What do you mean you're on your way there? You're in hospital.'

'I checked myself out.'

'Shit, Brennan. Do you know what you're doing?'

'No, but I don't have a choice. There's nobody else.'

'We'll be on standby. You've got twenty minutes to talk her down, after that, we come up, you understand me?'

But Jill had already hung up.

There were no spaces available when Jill drove into the car park behind the Kirkbride Complex, so she double-parked. She ran as fast as her body would allow, biting down on her lip to distract herself from the shooting pain across her ribs. She looked up at the tower but there was no sign of Fin. Three burly men from the security company were directing students away from the courtyard. Barriers had been set up.

The colour of the sky had changed. Cumulonimbus gathered on the horizon, tinted purple clouds were stirring and moving eastwards towards them.

'Hang on, love, not so fast,' said a man in a security uniform. Thunder rumbled in the distance.

Jill stopped and turned. 'Is she still up there?'

The security guard's face was firm. And who could blame him? She must look a sight with her tangled hair and battered and bruised face.

Jill flashed her ID. 'I'm Detective Jill Brennan, Chatswood Police.'

'Right, sorry, love. Yeah, she's still there.'

'How did she get into the tower?' Jill asked.

'She broke the lock. I guess she had a hammer. Whoever installed that lock should be shot. The lock's as flimsy as all shit.'

'How long has she been up there?'

'No more than an hour. I'd just started my shift when I thought I saw someone up there so I went to have a look see. When I saw the broken lock I went up. I thought it might have been some of the students skylarking. I was almost at the top when this woman pulled a gun on me.' He ran his hand roughly through his hair. 'I backed off quick smart. They don't pay me enough to take that kind of shit.'

'Have you called an ambulance?' Jill asked.

'They're on their way, should be here any minute. I told them not to use their sirens and stay back. I didn't call the police; she said she'd jump if I did. She said she only wanted to speak to Detective Brennan so I was waiting for you to turn up.'

Jill gave a nod and asked the guard for his Maglite, remembering how dark it was in the stairwell. She walked over to the tower and made her way up the narrow, stone steps. Jill held her ribs, remembered the doctor's warning about exerting herself.

When she reached the top, Fin was waiting for her. A packet of potato chips had fallen out from an open backpack and a hammer was lying on the floor at Fin's feet. Fin had a gun in her hand. Jill guessed it was Robbie's Glock.

Fin's eyes were unblinking. 'What happened to you?'

Jill put her hands in the air and took a step towards her. 'This is about you, Fin, not me.'

'Get back. You're too close. I fuckin' well mean it. I'll shoot you, don't think I won't.'

'Come on, Fin, put the gun down.' Jill took a step back. Let's try and sort this out. Just you and me, together.' While Jill waited for Fin to speak, she tried to work out what Fin's next move was going to be.

Fin seemed to relax a little. 'We can talk, but I'm not putting the gun down.'

'Whatever you want. Just stay nice and calm.' Jill knew there was no point making things any tenser than they already were, so she sat down on the stone floor with her legs out in front of her and leaned up against the damp wall. She took a shallow breath. 'Sit down, Fin, I don't like talking at different eye-levels.' Jill looked into Fin's eyes, there was clarity there and she seemed more composed than the previous times they'd spoken.

Fin sat down and crossed her legs as if she was preparing for a yoga class. She balanced the gun in her lap and pointed it at Jill. 'It was a mistake,' she said. 'It was all one big fucking mistake.' A shadow crossed Fin's face. 'I thought Adam was a friend. He gave me drugs sometimes when I was feeling lousy. One day when we were hanging out at the Interchange, he told me what his uncle's friends were doing to these kids they were picking up off the streets. The way he told me it was like he was a big man, like I'd be impressed or something. It made me sick.' A beat of silence. 'I told him about Uncle Patrick, how he abused me when I was a kid. What it felt like to be treated that way, how you never get over it. I told Adam what his Uncle was doing wasn't right and I was going to tell Robbie about it if he didn't get his uncle to stop. I still remember the look on Adam's face. I should have known what it meant. By the time I found out what was really going on, it was too late. Robbie was dead.'

'Tell me about Patrick,' Jill said.


Fin's fingers tightened around the trigger. 'Robbie told me he was going to give Uncle Patrick a good hiding for what he'd done to me and to our family, get him to pay us compensation, then he was going to make sure he went to prison.'

'Is that why Robbie moved to Glover Street? To be closer to Patrick.'

Fin nodded.

'When did Robbie find out about what Patrick had done to you?'

'We were still kids. I told him after Patrick left Katoomba and moved away. With him gone, I thought it was safe to tell Robbie. While Patrick was still living with us I was always worried what Robbie would do if he ever found out. Robbie would have started something, but Patrick was an adult...he would have finished it.'

'So what did happen when Robbie found out?'

'He went crazy.' Fin started breathing faster; she couldn't get enough air. 'He...he thought he'd let me down. I think that's why he joined the police; it was too late to save me, but he thought he could save others like me.'

'Why didn't you go to the police about Patrick when Robbie found him? All we needed was a statement. We would have investigated him, got a confession. He would have gone to prison for a very long time.'

'What? A statement from me? Who was going to believe me?' Fin looked down at the gun in her hand. 'I was only eight years old when Patrick started abusing me. At first he just cuddled me like I remembered my dad used to. I liked being close to him. I liked the smell of him and the way he told me he loved me. Then things changed, cuddles turned to other things. I used to think there was something wrong with me, that it was my fault that he did 'it' to me, like I needed to be punished.'

A stretch of silence.

'What about Patrick? Did you shoot him?' Jill's voice was quiet and low.

'I don't know, I don't remember.' Fin raised herself onto the ledge. 'When Gracie got sick, Robbie went to the Mountains to see her. Gracie told Robbie she'd promised not to report Patrick to the police if he moved away and never showed his face again. It was the only way she could get him out of the house and away from Robbie and me.'

'Did you know he'd changed his family name?'

Fin nodded. 'Robbie told me. Robbie found out he'd changed it from Reilly to Hill. I still can't believe Gracie made a deal with Uncle Patrick.'

'It might have had something to do with the family's reputation,' Jill said. 'It was a different time when you were growing up, people didn't like to talk about paedophilia, especially when a family member was involved.'

'Remember when I told you, you knew nothing about families?' Fin twisted her lips into a half-smile. 'Well, you don't know the half of it.'

Silence.

'What do you remember about the night Robbie died?' Jill asked.

The hurt and grief on Fin's face was palpable. She closed her eyes.

Jill held her ribs and tried to stand.

Fin's eyes flashed open. 'Sit down,' she screamed and waved the gun at Jill.

Jill sat.

'I can't remember much of what happened that night, okay? But I swear if I did push him, I didn't mean to, I was pissed, confused.' The wind whistled through the tower. Fin drew a deep breath, wiped her eyes. 'I phoned Robbie, told him I was in the tower and he had to come up and get me, or else I'd jump. I taunted him, made him climb the stairs even though I knew he was scared of heights. I was surprised he did it. He was standing where you are now. He told me it was time I learnt to take responsibility for my life. When I climbed up onto this ledge here, I told him I was going to jump; he tried to get me down.' Fin reached into the pocket of her jeans with her free hand and wrapped her fingers around the feathers she'd brought with her. 'I've been having these dreams. I think there was somebody else here but I don't know who it was. Thought it was Adam but it couldn't have been him because he was in hospital.'

'According to Adam it was one of Wan's men. And Robbie fell…you didn't push him.' Jill tried to reach out to Fin, but Fin raised the gun again.

'I must have blacked out, 'cause I can't remember any of that. One minute Robbie was standing there and...when I woke up I thought Robbie had gone home and left me here on my own, so I walked back down the steps and left. I had no idea he was lying down there on the ground.' Fin turned to look at the ground over her shoulder. She rubbed her temple with the gun barrel. 'I'm so tired.' Fin heard the words but couldn't work out how they were coming out of her mouth. Her lips felt like they were covered in some-thing heavy and sticky, like bubble gum. Where was she? Who was the woman sitting by the stairs? Robbie's friend? The detective?

Fin heard footsteps, voices. She ran the palm of her hand along the gun barrel. What was she saying, the woman with the bruised face? Her lips were moving but Fin couldn't make out the words. The woman was walking towards her, getting closer. So close. Just take one step, Fin. It will be over in a second. Fin watched the angel's feathers catch flight, taken up by the wind.

A scuttle of feet, strong arms reaching out.

'No! Fin! No!'

Fin Calloway fell into the sky.


Was it seconds? Minutes? Rimis was beside her, holding her, talking quietly to her, reassuring her.

Jill sobbed. Shook her head. 'I was talking to her...I thought I could bring her down. I tried to save her, but I couldn't.' Jill looked up into Rimis's eyes.

Rimis wrapped his arms around her. Jill leaned against him and punched her closed fists against his chest.

'She's gone, Jill. They're both gone. There's noth-ing you could have done for either of them.'

# FORTY-NINE

THE FINAL ACCOUNT OF OPERATION Warlord had taken almost ten days for Detective Inspector Scott Carver to write. He threw the signed report into his out-tray and leaned back in his office chair. It wasn't a lengthy or complicated report but Jill Brennan's unexpected involvement in the operation and the demands on his time over the past month in general had left him reeling. His feelings for her went much deeper than he realised.

He knew she could be reckless, but her tenaciousness and investigation into Robbie Calloway's death had ultimately led them to Vincent Wan. And he knew if it hadn't been for Fin Calloway's involvement with Adam Lee and Robbie's subsequent suspicions of him, Vincent Wan would still be at large.

On the other side of the city, Jill walked into Rimis's office and sat down in the visitor's chair. She tucked a stray lock of hair behind her ear and looked across the desk at Rimis. The last couple of weeks had taken their toll on her, not to mention Rimis. She looked at him. They both deserved and needed a holiday.

'What are you doing here? You're supposed to be on sick leave.' Rimis put his mug of coffee down and looked into Jill's tired eyes.

Jill leant over the desk and was about to say something, when Rimis put up his hand to stop her. 'Listen, I know what you're thinking. Adam Lee, right? We don't know what his involvement was, if any in Robbie's and Hill's deaths. Adam Lee was in North Shore Hospital the night Robbie died and he's got a rock-solid alibi for the night Hill died. A female friend said he was home all night with her. They watched a re-run of *Love Actually*. She gave Chapman a scene-by-scene run-down of the movie.'

'That doesn't mean anything. For a start, who's to say Lee was there? Besides, like me and another couple of hundred thousand women, she's probably watched that movie more than half a dozen times.'

Rimis looked at her. 'Really? I thought you were more the Bruce Willis, *Die Hard*, type, Brennan.'

She was about to have a go at him when the look on Rimis's face changed. 'We're holding Adam Lee on a list of charges a mile long. It should do for now.'

Jill tried to control her breathing, tried to stop the anger taking over. But she knew she'd have to settle for the lesser charges against Adam Lee. What else could she do?

# FIFTY

THE FOLLOWING MORNING JILL DROVE across town to Callan Park. The early Sunday morning traffic was light across the Anzac Bridge. Jill thought back to her short stay in hospital. After Fin had taken her life, Rimis had insisted she return to her hospital bed. She smiled when she thought of Scott Carver and Nick Rimis. They had been like schoolboys vying for her attention. They'd both arrived at the same time and brought flowers and chocolates from the team. Rawlings, Choi and Chapman had brought magazines and fruit. Bea, Harry and Callum had also come to visit, staying by her bedside, talking and watching television with her. She considered all of them family. But she still wanted, needed, more. She'd decided to apply for extended leave. Spain. It was time to go in search of her mother's family.

Jill pulled into the car park behind the Kirkbride Complex and sat for a long time before she got out. She was still angry with herself for not being able to save Fin and of course there was the lingering guilt over not returning Robbie's phone call. If she had called Robbie, it may have stopped the tragic chain of events that had led to four deaths: Robbie, Patrick Hill, Vincent Wan and Fin.

Jill found a place to sit in the grassy courtyard and pulled out a sketchpad, a black crayon pencil, and a small sheet of plastic from her backpack. The light was soft and hazy and the walls surrounding the courtyard provided protection from the wind. Jill's shoulders dropped and as the sketch took shape on the paper in front of her she started to relax.

Half an hour later she was done. She looked up, studied the tower and compared it with the sketch. It was a fair attempt. The decorative stonework moldings, the circular elements of the facades and the double-arch openings had been captured to her satisfaction. A copper ball and weather vein sat on top of the pyramid-shaped roof and she decided to leave the details to the end. Above the lintel was a date stone with MDCCCLXXX111 carved into it. She shifted her weight and resettled the sketchpad on her knees. She was thinking about the Roman numerals when she heard a familiar voice behind her.

'Might of known you'd be here.'

Jill dropped her sketchpad and turned around.

Rimis smiled and peered over her shoulder at the sketch. 'Not bad,' he said.

'What are you doing here?' Jill asked.

'Thought I'd take a look at this place in the daylight and under different circumstances.' Rimis looked up at the tower, then back to Jill. 'How are you feeling?'

'The bruising is fading, but my ribs still feel like I've been trapped in a cardboard compactor for the past week.' She went to pick up her backpack.

Rimis grabbed the backpack for her.

'I had a call from Greer. I was going to wait until tomorrow when you came into work to tell you, but I might as well tell you now.'

Jill raised her eyebrows.

'It's Fin's autopsy report. She was suffering from a condition called TLE, temporal lobe epilepsy.'

'I didn't see her have any fits,' Jill said. 'I thought the blackouts; loss of memory was to do with her heavy drinking.'

'With the kind of epilepsy Fin had, there isn't any jerking or loss of consciousness. According to Greer, it can cause changes in mood and personality, usually anger and rage. Also hallucinations.'

'What about her memory loss?'

'Apparently when the seizure happens, you can wake up with no memory of where you went or what you did. You can find yourself lost, or in an odd place or situation. The waking up happens when the seizure finishes. Greer told me of a case study she'd read. A woman with the condition drove up a motorway in the wrong direction and ploughed into a family sedan. The occupants of the van were all killed but she escaped injury. She had no memory of getting into the car.'

Jill noticed Rimis staring at the tower. She could only imagine what he was thinking.

'The sad part about it,' he said, 'is Fin may have responded to medication.'

Jill knew Rimis was a kind, sensitive man underneath his gruff exterior. He reminded her of a younger version of her father. She suddenly thought it sad that, like her, he had no other plans for a Sunday afternoon other than to revisit a crime scene. Although he'd called Doctor Ross Greer…again.

'How's Greer?' Jill let the question hang, fishing.

Rimis smiled, but then looked off into the distance.

Jill would never get an answer…or maybe she just had.

They stood in silence, taking in the gardens for a few minutes.

Rimis cleared his throat and turned to her. 'Do you ever regret joining the force?' Rimis asked.

'I've always felt it was the right decision.' But after recent events, Jill wasn't so sure anymore. She let her head fall back and looked up at the sky. It was good to see the sun again after so much rain.

'Feel like a walk?' Rimis asked.

Jill nodded. The grass was lush; the pale blue sky was furrowed with wispy bands of clouds.

'After all that's happened here, it's still a beautiful place,' Rimis said. Jill agreed with him and for a moment she tried to imagine Callan Park, as it once must have been when good people with good intentions designed it. The open fields sloping down to Iron Cove Bay with man-made lakes filled with ducks and swans, vegetable gardens, tennis courts. There had even been a piggery once.

They walked together enjoying each other's company without talking. They came to a tall sandstone wall.

'Do you know what they call this?' Jill asked.

'A sandstone wall?'

Jill smiled. 'It's called a 'Ha-Ha' wall. It's a landscaping device. It was used to provide views of the landscape beyond. Patients felt secure without feeling enclosed. Maybe that was why Fin was drawn to the tower. Like the Jacaranda tree when she was a little girl; she felt safe.' Jill needed to find somewhere where she felt safe. Somewhere she could see the world in a better light.

Jill took her backpack from Rimis and they walked together across the grounds. The mid-morning light filtered through the leaves of the trees and as she looked back at the tower, she thought of Robbie and Fin, whose lives she was unable to save, and Adam Lee and Vincent Wan. She had to let them all go. It was time to get on with her life.

# Acknowledgements

I would like to acknowledge the past patients and staff of Callan Park Mental Hospital (later known as Rozelle Hospital).

Special thanks to friends and family who supported and encouraged me in the writing of this book. I am indebted to Phillipa Martin for her expert editorial services, her wise counsel and patience during the many drafts of the manuscript.

A special thank you to Doctor Coletta Hobbs and Doctor Christopher Lauer for allowing me to 'pick their brains' in all matters relating to psychology and pathology, respectively. I enjoyed the conversations!

I would also like to thank Kerry Rogerson for assisting me with police procedures and putting up with my relentless questions during odd hours both day and night.

Also thank you for the forensic information so generously shared by Doctor Doug Lyle.

*Asylum* is a work of fiction. The clock tower in the grounds of the Kirkbride Complex is not accessible to the general public. Kirkbride is occupied by Sydney University of the Arts and is private property.

I apologise for the liberties I took with police procedures and please forgive any medical, historical, geographical errors or omissions, which were made purely in the interests of dramatic fiction.

# ABOUT THE AUTHOR

Gina Amos grew up in the Hunter Valley, a one and a half hour drive north of Sydney. She now lives in the Gold Coast. Gina is married with two wonderful children and aside from writing, she enjoys travelling the world, reading, swimming, boating and spending time with family and friends.

Her first novel, in the Detective Jill Brennan series, *Secrets and Lies* was self-published in 2011 followed by *Killing Sunday* in 2014. *Asylum* is the third novel in the series.

·